Praise for Sixties Girl

"Stories from the Swinging Sixties help friends overcome their divisions and a family bridge the generation gap in this uplifting contemporary tale. Young readers will identify with Will's insecurities, and cheer when he realizes goodness surrounds him. When in doubt, Grandma's story box has the answer."

HARRIET ZAIDMAN, author of *Second Chances,* winner of the Geoffrey Bilson Award for Historical Fiction for Young People

"In this thoughtful middle-grade novel, the past deftly intersects with the present. His grandmother's old suitcase, stuffed with random objects, becomes eleven-year-old Will's portal to both family and world history, and to a better understanding of himself. An empowering book about sharing stories, *Sixties Girl* is sure to stimulate conversation between generations."

GABRIELE GOLDSTONE, award-winning author of family-inspired novels *Crow Stone* and *Tainted Amber*

"Listening to stories told by his grandmother about growing up in the 1960s compels young Will to ask hard questions about his own relationships with friends and family. Heartfelt, warm, rich in details, meticulously researched, and complete with intriguing historical notes, MaryLou Driedger's *Sixties Girl* adeptly brings the era to life."

LARRY VERSTRAETE, author of *Coop the Great*

D1500116

"MaryLou Driedger has deftly woven together a historical fiction story of a girl growing up in the fast-changing 1960s and a contemporary story of a boy dealing with bullying, making new friends, and learning how to trust. Both storylines are compelling in their own right, and together they form this beautifully written novel that lets us sink into each character's coming-of-age journey. *Sixties Girl* is a captivating page turner that I did not want to end! Fans of Driedger's first book, *Lost on the Prairie*, will not be disappointed!"

JODI CARMICHAEL, award-winning author of *The U-nique Lou Fox*

Sixties Girl

MaryLou Driedger

WANDERING FOX

An imprint of
HERITAGE HOUSE PUBLISHING
Victoria | Vancouver | Calgary

Wandering Fox Books, an imprint of
Heritage House Publishing Company Ltd.
heritagehouse.ca

Cataloguing information available from Library and Archives Canada
978-1-77203-435-6 (paperback)
978-1-77203-436-3 (e-book)

Edited by Deborah Froese
Copyedited by Nandini Thaker
Cover and interior design by Setareh Ashrafologhalai

The interior of this book was produced on 100% post-consumer
paper, processed chlorine free, and printed with vegetable-based inks.

Heritage House gratefully acknowledges that the land on which we
live and work is within the traditional territories of the Lkwungen
(Esquimalt and Songhees), Malahat, Pacheedaht, Scia'new, T'Sou-ke,
and W̱SÁNEĆ (Pauquachin, Tsartlip, Tsawout, Tseycum) Peoples.

We acknowledge the financial support of the Government of
Canada through the Canada Book Fund (CBF) and the Canada Council
for the Arts, and the Province of British Columbia through the
British Columbia Arts Council and the Book Publishing Tax Credit.

27 26 25 24 23   1 2 3 4 5

Printed in Canada

*To my sister, Kaaren, and
my brothers, Ken and Mark*

Contents

1

I Don't Need a Babysitter

WILL

"YOU ARE definitely not staying here alone after school and that's final." Dad sounds like he's arguing one of his cases in court.

"Why? I'm totally responsible." I fight to calm my voice. "My teacher used that exact word to describe me on my last report card—*responsible*."

Dad tosses one of his tennis balls up in the air and catches it. "That's not the point, Will. Manitoba law says you need to be twelve to stay home alone, and in this house, we obey the law."

"But I don't have to be alone. Emmaline and Aneesh can come over," I protest.

"Is either of your friends twelve years old?" Dad asks.

"No." I push my glasses up my nose, straighten my shoulders, and try a different tactic. "Alex isn't twelve and he stays by himself after school."

Mom looks up from her computer. "Your cousin Alex lives in Vancouver. Rules are different in British Columbia. Besides, this arrangement with Grandma is only for Wednesdays when I have to teach a late afternoon class at the university."

"I KNOW! And Wednesday is the only day during the week my friends can hang out after school."

"It's just for a few months," Mom says.

"I'm not some kid anymore." I am almost shouting. "Sheesh! I've even taken the babysitter course and now you're telling me *I* need a babysitter!"

Mom snaps her computer shut. "Your grandmother isn't really a babysitter, Will. You liked spending time at her house when she lived in Rocky Creek. Now that she's moved into an apartment just down the street, it's so convenient for you to go there."

"Wouldn't it be even more *convenient* for me to stay here for a couple of hours after school? I could do helpful stuff like take out the trash or clean my room."

Mom laughs. "Now you sound desperate, Will."

I *am* desperate. Emmaline and Aneesh and I always get together on Wednesdays. It's the only day none of us has music or art lessons or soccer practice. What am I going to tell them? We can't hang out because I have to stay with Grandma? No way! They think I don't have a grandmother.

It's not like I actually lied to them about it. I just didn't correct them when they assumed my grandparents had died.

Dad picks up his tennis racquet and heads towards our front door. "The case is closed, Will. We will revisit our decision in November when you turn twelve."

Great. That's more than twelve weeks away.

ANEESH AND Emmaline are waiting for me on the bleachers by the basketball court on the first Wednesday of my sentence. We always meet there after school and walk home together. It's usually the best part of my day, but right now I'm shaky and anxious.

"Yikes! It's so cold and its only September." Aneesh sets his trombone case on the bench beside him and pulls a Winnipeg Jets toque over his straight black hair. "Not many weeks left till concert band tryouts, Will. Are you nervous?"

"Making the band will be a cinch for both of you," Emmaline says.

I play the tuba and Emmaline loves to listen in when Aneesh and I have a jam session.

"I don't think making the band will be a cinch, Emmaline, but I sure hope I get in." I slow my pace as we reach the supermarket on the corner. It's where I have to turn to go to Grandma's. I don't want Emmaline and Aneesh to know that I haven't really been honest about her, so I stumble over my rehearsed excuse. "Hey... uh, guys... I've got to... pick up some stuff at the store. Dad's making enchiladas for supper."

"Should we come in with you?" It's so cold Emmaline's nose is starting to turn as red as her hair.

"No! Uh . . . no. I'll be fine. You two should go to Aneesh's like we planned and warm up."

"Okay." Aneesh shifts his trombone to his other hand. "Come by later if you want to join us for some video games, Will."

"Hope the enchiladas are good." Emmaline tightens the string on her yellow hoodie. "If you have leftovers, bring them to share for lunch tomorrow."

I nod and wave good-bye, scurrying into the store. I pace the aisles till I'm sure my friends will be long gone. Then I head back out the door without buying anything.

I wish I'd told Aneesh and Emmaline the truth about Grandma right from the beginning. Last year, when Aneesh talked about a video call with his grandparents in India, Emmaline said he was lucky. She didn't have any grandparents. They looked at me, and Emmaline asked, "What about you, Will?"

I didn't answer because who my grandmother *is* had caused me a lot of problems in the past. My silence gave them the wrong impression, though. Aneesh put his hand on my shoulder and said, "That's too bad, Will."

I didn't correct him. Looking back now, I wish I had.

Aneesh and Emmaline are the best friends ever. I don't want to lose them. So I'm going into stealth mode on Wednesdays.

TEN MINUTES later, I'm outside Grandma's apartment block. I scan the street. When I'm sure nobody I know is walking by, I quickly punch in the code to open the front doors. They stay closed.

What's up with that? Do I have the numbers wrong?

I would have saved the code for Grandma's door in my phone, except I don't have one. My parents not only think I'm too young to stay home alone on Wednesdays, they also think I'm too young to have a phone. I dig through my backpack looking for the paper where Grandma wrote the door code down for me.

I toss the mustardy crusts from my pastrami sandwich onto the apartment steps, then my stinky soccer cleats. I'm still rummaging through my backpack when a smooth wet tongue licks my hand. I jerk my head up. A brown and white basset hound with wrinkly skin sits in front of me.

"Sorry about that," says a deep rumbling voice.

I wipe my hand on my sweatpants and follow the dog's leash to a very tall man in a bright red sweater.

"Mendelssohn caught the scent of your bread crusts and thought he'd say hello," the man says. "I apologize for him slobbering all over your hand. Are you visiting someone in the building?"

"My grandmother. Laura Johnson."

"Well, that's a coincidence. She lives just across the hall from me. I can let you in the front door. My name is Leon, by the way."

"I'm Will Sanders."

As we cross the lobby to the elevator, Mendelssohn stares up at me with these huge eyes, as if he's trying to figure out what I'm doing here.

Join the club, I feel like saying.

Leon presses the elevator button for the sixth floor. "Lucky you, Will, to have such a wonderful storyteller like Laura Johnson in the family."

I wish she wasn't a storyteller, I think to myself.

"She's written so many books," Leon continued. "When I was a kid, I loved the one about the little boy who took off all his clothes in the art gallery."

"You mean *Why Are You Naked*?"

Leon nods. "Such a great story."

I don't say anything to Leon, but I wish Grandma had NEVER written that book. I shudder. Couldn't she at least have picked a less embarrassing title?

The kids at my old elementary school found out Laura Johnson was my Grandma when I made the mistake of bringing one of her picture books to class. She had written a message inside: *To my special grandson, Will.* My grade four teacher happened to see it and told practically the whole school about all the books for little kids my grandmother had written. Everyone started asking annoying questions about her. But the worst part? It gave more ammunition to Gregory and Grayson, the two boys on my school soccer team who had been teasing me about how skinny I was and what an ugly sound my tuba made.

Grayson liked to knock off my hat. "Look at Will's hair. He could be the *princess* in his grandma's book, *The Curly-Haired Princess.*"

Gregory, the bigger one, would say, "Will's like that wimpy kid in his grandma's book, *Stuck in the Mud.* Except he's not stuck in the mud! He's stuck behind those goofy glasses!" Then he'd grab my glasses and threaten to break them.

It just got worse from there. Like, *way* worse. Gregory and Grayson made my life miserable. I didn't want to go to school. I should have told Mom and Dad about it, but there was no way I wanted Grandma to find out. If she'd known I was getting bullied because of her books, she would have felt terrible.

I was glad when we moved across the city last year and I started grade five at Helen Armstrong Middle School. No one knew me there. It was the perfect opportunity to avoid the problem altogether by making sure no one found out *who* my grandmother was or that I even had one.

Don't get me wrong. I love my grandma. It's just complicated.

BEFORE I can knock, Grandma opens her apartment door. "Hi, William." She wraps me in one of her squeeze-as-tight-as-you-can hugs. I'm probably getting too old for them, but I don't have the heart to tell her.

"I've got raisin cookies and chocolate milk on the table." Grandma's voice rises over the sound of her buzzing cell phone. She looks down at the number. "I have to take this, William. It's the people publishing my next book."

Grandma calls me "William." It's pretty old-fashioned and makes me sound like some ancient guy with a moustache. I've told my parents under no circumstances are they ever to call me William. But Grandma likes it because it was her dad's name. I figure it's okay for a kid to cut his grandmother a little slack when it comes to something like that.

I grab a cookie and wander into the study, where a huge desk takes up most of the room. All of Grandma's books are lined up on a long shelf just above it. Their colorful spines dance with the funny titles that little kids love so much.

I pull one of the books off the shelf and flip it over to check the author photo on the back cover. Grandma and I both have grey-green eyes, a slightly crooked front tooth, and curly brown hair. Hers is shoulder length but mine is super short. Mom made me get it cut for the first day of school.

The walls in Grandma's study are jammed floor to ceiling with family photos. Lots are of Grandpa, who died less than a year ago, but there are also plenty of me and my cousin Alex with our parents.

I spot an old suitcase in the corner. It's plastered with colorful stickers and a big label in Grandma's handwriting that says STORIES. Curious, I click open the silver latch and lift the lid. A jumble of random things is crammed inside. I pull out a faded board for a game called Parcheesi. I'm still messing around in the suitcase looking for game movers or dice when Grandma comes into the study.

"I see you've found my story suitcase, William."

I look up, blushing. "Sorry. I should have asked before I opened it."

Grandma smiles. "I don't mind at all. Did you find anything interesting?"

"There's lots of strange stuff here, Grandma. What's Parcheesi?"

"It's a racing game. That particular one was a gift from a nun dressed up like Santa Claus. I got it when I was six and our family was living in Winnipeg."

"I've read about nuns in books. Maybe seen a couple in movies. But I'm pretty sure I've never actually met one."

"When I was a girl in the sixties, I saw nuns everywhere. Thousands of them were nurses and teachers here in Winnipeg."

"That's weird."

"It sometimes was. Are you interested in hearing more about it?"

"May as well, Grandma. Have to stay here till supper time anyway."

"Then I'll tell you a story about something that happened to me when I was in grade one and every teacher in my school was a nun."

2

Wet Pants

LAURA, 1960

I'D WET my pants. I was sure all the other passengers were staring at me, so I kept my eyes glued to the floor.

I'd been taking the same city bus home from school for almost a year, so Mr. Calvez, the regular driver, had become my friend. He must have the noticed the river of pee twisting along the floor. When he pulled up at a red light, he turned to look at me in my usual spot in the seat right behind him.

"Laura, do you need some help?"

"No. Thanks," I mumbled. I didn't want to be rude, but I wished Mr. Calvez would just drive and not pay any attention to me today.

The windshield wipers on the bus swished back and forth in perfect rhythm like the metronome on Mom's piano. I'd had the worst day ever in grade one and was oh so close to bursting into tears. I tried to focus on the raisin cookie and chocolate milk I knew would be waiting for me at home. Just thinking about them made me feel better.

My day had started out pretty smoothly but got turned upside down in the lunchroom. There wasn't space for me at the table with the kids from the English classes, so I had to sit with the students who spoke French. I couldn't understand a thing they were saying. Since it was Friday, Mom had made a tuna sandwich. She knew I didn't like to be different than all the Catholic kids in my school who always ate fish on Fridays, but tuna was not my favourite. I decided to wash my sandwich down with more orange Kool-Aid.

I was just pouring another cup from my Thermos when this horrible boy named Clement pinched me—hard! I jumped. The Thermos slid out of my hand, landing on the floor with a tremendous bang. It smashed into pieces along with all my happy feelings about the day so far.

Sister Angeline, who was in charge of the lunchroom, sailed over to where I was sitting. "Did you just make a noise?" she screeched, her face turning purple. "You know the rules, Laura. Absolute silence is to be maintained—"

"But I dropped my Thermos because Clement—"

"Don't interrupt and don't make excuses." Sister Angeline pointed to my shattered Thermos. "Pick up that mess and put it in the trash bin. Then go and stand in the corner with your face to the wall."

I obeyed.

Sister Angeline kept coming over to check on me. Each time she'd give a loud, disapproving sniff. Then she'd pull out the wooden clapper tucked into the pocket of her habit, hold it up to my ear, and click it. It sounded like an alligator's teeth snapping. All the nuns in our school had clappers. Sometimes, if we were really naughty they would nip the tips of our ears with them.

The bell rang for class to start. Sister Angeline stopped me as I left the lunchroom. "Laura, it is very important for nice young ladies to learn to be quiet and not draw attention to themselves." She went on and on, reminding me of all the ways I could improve my behaviour. Her little lecture meant I didn't have time to go to the washroom before I went back to class. I was already late.

As I slipped into my desk, my teacher, Sister Odile, peered at me over her wire-frame glasses and frowned. "Being on time is important, Laura. I'll expect you to do better in the future."

I wanted to scream, *It isn't my fault I'm late!* But that would only get me into even more trouble.

We couldn't go out for recess in the afternoon because it was raining buckets. Sister Odile decided to give us an addition test instead. Math was hard for me but I knew all my facts because I'd practised them at home every night with Mom. Before I could finish my test, Sister Odile's habit swished like a whirlwind as she bustled by my desk. She snatched my math paper away from me. I looked up.

"Time for you to go in the hall, Laura."

While I'd been busy with my test, the priest had arrived to teach the Catholic kids about their First Communion, which would take place next year. He stood at the front of the room in his long black robe, tapping his right foot as fast as a telegraph operator's finger. His face reminded me of the impatient bear who'd clawed the window of the cottage we'd rented at Windward Lake last summer.

Since I wasn't Catholic, my parents had asked I be excused from the priest's lessons. That meant when he arrived, I was banished to a rickety desk in the hall. I flipped through the boring Dick and Jane books the teacher had left for me to read. I tried to imagine what the priest was saying to my classmates that my parents didn't want me to hear. Was it scary?

The girls had been talking about the frilly white dresses their moms were going to sew for their First Communion. My Mom sewed dresses for me, but I'd never had a real fancy one.

I wished there was at least one other kid in the class who wasn't Catholic, someone who could sit in the hall with me. I was lonely, and to make matters worse, I *really* needed to go to the bathroom. All that orange Kool-Aid was sloshing around inside me.

I knew it was wrong to use the bathroom without permission from my teacher, but Sister Odile was in the classroom. I sure wasn't about to go in there and interrupt the priest. I crossed my legs tightly and shifted my bum on the creaky seat of the desk.

I wished as hard as I could that the priest would leave, but he stayed and stayed. I watched the hands on the big hallway clock crawl towards the end of the school day. By the time the priest left the classroom, I *really, really* had to go, but if I went to the bathroom now, I would miss my usual bus. Then I'd have to stand in the rain for a long time waiting for the next one, and I'd get home late. Mom would be terribly worried. So instead of heading towards the washroom, I caught the bus.

MR. CALVEZ turned on the blinker and pulled into the driveway of the St. Boniface Hospital. We lived on the grounds in a special apartment building with the families of other people studying to be doctors like my dad.

"You're home, Laura," Mr. Calvez said gently. He waved as I got off the bus, the pee still trickling down my legs and soaking into my white bobby socks. The rain drenched my uniform as I ran all the way from the bus stop to our building, eager for a hug from Mom, a raisin cookie, and my chocolate milk.

I flung open the apartment door to find our home full of kids. Mom sometimes babysat for our neighbour Melba. Her three children were playing tag with my four-year-old sister, Marjorie. They were all darting around our tiny living room like goldfish in a bowl.

"You're it," Marjorie shouted as she tapped one of the kids.

My baby brother, Frankie, his mouth a big, round letter O outlined with crumbs, giggled in his highchair as he watched the circus. I glanced at the kitchen table, messy with bits of raisin cookies and half-finished glasses of chocolate milk.

The cookie plate was empty.

"Did they eat all the cookies?" I screamed, my face on fire. Everyone froze and turned to stare at me.

Mom came to the door and crouched down so she could look into my teary eyes. "What in the world is going on, Laura?"

The story of my day gushed out between sobs and hiccups. Mom listened and then took my hand, leading me into the bathroom. She filled the tub with warm water and sprinkled in the Dreft laundry detergent she used on little Frankie's clothes. Balloons of foam rose as she whisked my uniform over my head and stripped off my socks and shoes. I slid into the bed of bubbles.

"Just soak for a bit, Laura." Mom shut the bathroom door. I could hear from the conversation outside that Melba had come to pick up her kids.

I felt like a queen there in the tub, all by myself. I had seen Queen Elizabeth last July when she visited Winnipeg. Dad took me up on the hospital rooftop, where I had a bird's eye view of her riding by in a black convertible. Looking through Dad's binoculars, the queen seemed so close to me that I could see her tiny pearl earrings. I watched as she waved to the sea of people packed ten deep on Tache Avenue.

I raised my arm out of the bubbles in the tub and pivoted it at my elbow. I waved elegantly at the rusty sink and the stinky pail full of Frankie's diapers.

A few minutes later, Mom came in with my favourite pair of blue pedal pushers and a white shirt. She laid them on the closed toilet lid. "I saved a raisin cookie for you, Laura. You can have it with your chocolate milk whenever you're ready." She shut the door.

When I got out of the bathroom, Marjorie was building something with the Lincoln Logs she'd dumped out on the kitchen table. "Does this look like the cottage at Windward Lake, Laura?"

"It looks exactly like it." I patted Marjorie on the shoulder.

Frankie was crawling around on the floor exploring for fallen cookie crumbs.

"How's the best brother in the world?" I gave him a kiss. I'd been so mad after school that I'd forgotten to do that.

When I'd finished my cookie and milk, Mom motioned for me to follow her into the bedroom. She scooped Frankie up and plopped him into his crib near the window, where he could watch us. We settled ourselves on the bed with our backs against the wooden headboard.

Mom straightened the seams of her stockings. "I know you had an awful day, Laura. Are you feeling better?"

"Lots better. But there *is* something I've been wondering about."

"What's that?"

"When I left school today, I didn't ever want to see another nun."

Mom put her arm around my shoulders. "And have you changed your mind?"

"Not exactly, but I have been thinking about that big party we went to at Christmas."

"You mean the party the nuns who work at the hospital hosted for the kids who live in our building?"

"Yes. They put up the tallest tree with a sparkling star on top and served cupcakes smothered in chocolate icing and bottles of 7up"

Mom nodded. "One nun was dressed up like Santa and handed out gifts. You sat on her knee. She gave you the Parcheesi game you'd been wanting."

"I know. The nuns at the party were really, really nice, but the ones at my school always seem grouchy and impatient. Why?"

"What do you think, Laura?"

I chewed my bottom lip for a minute. "Grandpa Peter says there are all kinds of people in this world. I guess that goes for nuns too."

3

Playing Parcheesi

WILL

I BUMP into Emmaline on the school steps the next Wednesday morning. I'm trying to juggle my tuba and the display board for my social studies project on the history of soccer, so she opens the door for me.

"Thanks, Emmaline."

"No problem."

I grin. "You're looking extra happy this morning. It bet it's because the first thing on the timetable is art."

"You know me pretty well, Will. Hey, do you and Aneesh want to come over after school to see the new mural I'm painting on my bedroom wall? We could play a few rounds of speed chess too."

I start to sweat and my chest feels tight. "I... uh... I don't think that will work. I'm having, uhm... an extra tuba lesson to get ready for concert band tryouts. I can't get together with you today."

I still haven't told Emmaline and Aneesh the truth about Grandma or Wednesdays. It's too late now. And it's better if no one knows about her anyway. There are bullies at Helen Armstrong too. I'm pretty sure Emmaline and Aneesh would stick up for me if anything bad happened, but then, I thought my friends at my old school would do that too. And they didn't. In fact, they even ...

I shudder. The whole thing makes me feel like throwing up and I don't want to think about it.

GRANDMA AND I play a game of Parcheesi at the kitchen table on my second visit. It's way more fun than I thought it would be. While we play, I ask about stuff in her wet pants story. "Why did the kids at your school have to be totally quiet when they ate lunch?"

"In the sixties, lots of people still believed children should be seen and not heard."

"Whoa! My school cafeteria usually sounds like a zoo at lunch."

"That's probably better than the deadly silence I experienced." Grandma edges her Parcheesi mover four spaces forward.

I hold the pair of dice in my hand before throwing them again. "At my old school, there were some really mean kids just like that guy Clement who made you break your

Thermos. My teachers were nice, though. I'm glad I didn't have to put up with difficult teachers too, like you did.

Grandma puts a hand on my arm. "People who are unkind are always tough to deal with, William, no matter how old you are, or how old they are."

I get all shaky inside, thinking about Gregory and Grayson. A tight feeling squeezes my chest, and for a split-second, I can't breathe.

After I win the Parcheesi game, I pack it up to return it to the story suitcase. I turn around at the study door. "Grandma, do you have a picture of your dad? You mentioned him in your story, but I don't know much about him except I've got his name."

"There should be a snapshot in the suitcase."

I find an awesome newspaper photo of my great-grandfather in an operating room. The caption says, *Doctor William Johnson doing surgery at Rocky Creek Hospital.* There's another newspaper clipping tucked into a corner of the suitcase.

"Wow! This car drove right into someone's living room, Grandma!" I say as I return to the kitchen and show her the clipping.

"That happened next door to my house."

"Weren't you living in your St. Boniface Hospital apartment anymore?

"No. My Dad got his first job as a doctor so we moved to a house on Beaverbrook Street in another part of Winnipeg. I was in grade two and went to Sir John Franklin School. I'd made friends with a neighbour girl named June. We both saw that accident." Grandma's voice drops and her eyes glisten.

"Grandma, you don't have to talk about it if you don't want to."

"I want to, William, and it's a story I think you're ready to hear. I've noticed how mature you're becoming."

I almost say, *Tell my parents that*. Instead, I sit back down at the kitchen table to hear Grandma's story.

4

A Car in the Living Room

LAURA, 1960

"ONE, TWO, THREE, JUMP!"

June and I had stopped on our way to school to play in a huge pile of leaves on the boulevard in front of the house next to mine.

"What are you girls doing? I just raked those leaves! Look at the mess you've made," Mrs. Withers, my neighbour, barked at us from her open front door. Her hair stuck up on her head in curly towers, like the ones in the crystal gardens we were growing at school with ammonia and laundry bluing.

"Good morning, Mrs. Withers," June and I chorused. Mom said we needed to be polite to her.

"What's good about it?" Mrs. Withers grunted and rubbed her back as she plodded over to the caragana hedge to pick up her copy of the *Winnipeg Free Press*. "That news-boy has terrible aim," she snapped. Her sour face made my lips pucker the way they did when I took a bite of one of Grandma Annie's dill pickles.

"Oh, look." June pointed to the open door where Mrs. Withers' son, Ronnie, stood facing us now. "He has nothing on but his underwear."

We giggled as Ronnie scratched the hair under his arms. His face was red, and his nose was swollen like he had a bad cold. "Ma, I need you!"

"What are you two looking at?" Mrs. Withers' voice crackled like the radio did when we couldn't find a station to listen to. "You get to school now."

"Such a sourpuss," I whispered to June.

"My mother says it's because she's had a hard life."

"What do you mean?" I asked as June and I looked both ways before crossing Lanark Avenue.

"Mom told me Mrs. Withers' husband was captured by the Nazis when he was in the army. They shot him. He's buried in Europe somewhere."

"That's horrible!" I shuddered.

"Mrs. Withers needed money to look after Ronnie when her husband died, so she got a job at a canning factory. Mrs. Withers had to stand all day working there, and it made her feet crooked."

I felt my face warm. I'd laughed at Mrs. Withers when she shuffled down to the Tomboy Store in her plaid bedroom slippers. Now I knew why she walked funny. "Poor Ronnie. He was just a kid like us when his father got killed," I say.

June nodded. Her voice softened as if she were telling me a secret. "I heard my parents talking one night. They said Ronnie has a drinking problem."

"What's a drinking problem?"

"It's when you drink lots of wine and beer and act strange," June informed me.

"My Grandpa Peter makes wine. I get a sip at Christmas. It doesn't make *me* act strange," I said.

"Well, it makes Ronnie act strange and sometimes he even gets angry, and he's not nice to his mother. Dad says his drinking problem is why he lost his job at the post office."

June and I reached Sir John Franklin School just when the bell rang. Sir John Franklin was an explorer who went to the North Pole and never came back. Like Ronnie's dad went to war and never came back.

Miss O'Shay was our grade two teacher. As we settled into our desks, June whispered, "Just look at Miss O'Shay's navy shoes. They match her dress perfectly."

Miss O'Shay clapped her hands. When she had our attention, she said, "Tomorrow there is no school because it's Remembrance Day. We'll attend a special assembly this afternoon. I want the boys to change into white shirts and ties when they go home for lunch. You girls wear your navy tunics with the Sir John Franklin crest. I need you to look your best when we recite the poem "In Flanders Fields" at the assembly. Now, let's stand beside our desks and practise it."

We repeated the poem perfectly. When we finished, the class was all quiet for just a second. It felt kind of magical, but then Billy McMillan spoiled it. "Is Flanders Fields even a real place?" he blurted out.

Miss O'Shay picked up the globe on her desk and pointed to a country in Europe. "Flanders Fields is in Belgium, Billy. A thousand Canadian soldiers are buried there."

I leaned toward June and whispered, "I wonder where Ronnie's father is buried?"

After our spelling lesson, Miss O'Shay gave us a picture to colour—a cross covered with poppies. While I made the poppies different shades of red, I thought about Ronnie Withers. It would be very sad to have your father die when you were just a kid and never see him again. My Dad worked so hard. We sometimes didn't see him for days, but we always knew he was coming home.

After recess, instead of reading us a chapter from *The Cricket in Times Square* like she usually did, Miss O'Shay said she had something special to show us.

"When I was in grade two, my father was in the Canadian army in Holland. I wrote him letters about what I was doing in Winnipeg. Dad saved the letters and brought them home in 1945 when the war was over. I want to read some to you."

As Miss O'Shay carefully pulled the first letter out of its yellowed envelope, I wondered if Ronnie wrote letters to his father when he was away. I wondered what had happened to those letters. Were they buried with Mr. Withers?

In one letter, Miss O'Shay told her father about learning to add big numbers in school. We were doing that too! I glanced at the tobacco tins lined up on the shelf under the window. They had once belonged to Miss O'Shay's father. Now they held coloured pegs that we could use to figure out hard math questions.

In another letter, my teacher described a new skipping game she'd learned from her friends at recess. One included a picture she'd drawn of a snowman. Each letter ended with her telling her Dad how much she missed him.

Miss O'Shay showed us a photograph of her father. He looked important in his dark blue army uniform with shiny buttons. "My Dad still keeps this uniform in his closet, even though it smells a bit like mothballs by now."

"Did your father win any medals?" Billy asked. "My grandpa did. He was in France in the Air Force. He was brave and—"

"My aunt Irene was brave too," June interrupted. "She was in the army."

"You're lying!" Billy's face got red. "Girls can't be soldiers."

Miss O'Shay pointed to the picture of Queen Elizabeth hanging above the blackboard. "Queen Elizabeth was in the army. She was a mechanic and drove a first aid truck."

I remembered watching the queen drive down Tache Avenue when she came to Winnipeg. After seeing her in a fancy hat and pearl earrings, it was hard to imagine her in an army uniform.

One by one, the other students told stories about a relative who had been in the army. I shuffled my feet and played with my pencil. I was usually the first kid to jump into class discussions, but I had nothing to say. I didn't know of anyone in my family who had been in the army.

Going home for lunch, June and I pretended we were soldiers. We marched down Beaverbrook Street swinging our arms and singing "O Canada." We arrived at Mrs. Withers' house just when we got to the line "in all our sons' command." June and I saluted each other, then she headed home.

I looked into Mrs. Withers' living room window. She was sitting in her rocking chair with her chin sagging on her chest. She seemed to be sleeping.

When I walked into the kitchen at home, Mom had Lipton's chicken noodle soup and a ham sandwich ready for me. The crusts were trimmed off, just the way I liked. Frankie sat in his highchair, gnawing the crusts and drooling. Marjorie held her doll on her lap and pretended to feed her some soup.

"How was school this morning?" Mom asked me the same question every day at lunch.

I told her about Miss O'Shay's letters and the other kids' stories. "Was anyone in our family in the war, Mom?"

"My big brother Herman stayed home instead of going into the army. He was Grandpa Peter and Grandma Annie's only son. The government thought it was just as important for him to help out on our farm as it was for him to fight."

"How come?"

"Canadian farmers had to keep growing food so it could be sent overseas to the soldiers fighting and the people in England starving because of the war."

"You mean people actually died because they didn't have enough to eat?" I asked.

"It was very sad, Laura."

"Didn't the food sometimes get bad by the time it got across the ocean? Miss O'Shay told us her father went to Europe on a boat. It was a long trip."

"Lots of the food was shipped overseas in cans."

"Mrs. Withers next door worked in a canning factory during the war, Mom. Does that mean she put food in cans for soldiers and starving people?"

"Yes, it does."

"Mrs. Withers had a really important job," I marvelled in between slurps of soup.

Mom took Frankie upstairs and put him down for his nap while Marjorie and I finished eating.

I brought my dishes to the counter, and just when I got there, a deafening crash filled the air. I jumped, and my soup bowl slipped out of my hand. It shattered in the sink the same way my Thermos had shattered last year in the school lunchroom.

"What was that?" Mom rushed down the stairs and ran to the living room window. "Oh no!" she screamed.

"What is it, Mom?" Marjorie and I raced into the living room.

"I need to call for help!" Mom sprang to the phone hanging on the hallway wall and dialed some numbers. "This is an emergency. There has been a terrible accident at 280 Beaverbrook Street. We need an ambulance immediately." She hung up the receiver and turned to me. "Laura, you stay right here. Keep your brother and sister inside." She hurried out the front door, slamming it shut behind her.

Marjorie and I charged to the window to see what had happened.

A blue car had smashed right into Mrs. Withers' living room!

I gasped. Mrs. Withers had been sleeping by the window when I came home for lunch. What if the car had hit her?

Marjorie whimpered. She grabbed my hand and held it tight.

I pressed my nose to the glass. June's father came running from down the street. He and Mom opened the car door. Mrs. Withers' son, Ronnie, fell out. Poppy-red blood stained his shirt and pants and washed over his face.

Frankie's wailing drew me away from the window. I went to his room and nearly tripped as I carried him back downstairs. He was two years old now and getting heavy. I shoved the old, embroidered hassock over to the window for Frankie to stand on. The three of us stared at the flashing lights of the police cars and ambulances as they arrived, their sirens blaring.

"Fire truck! Fire truck!" Frankie shouted, pointing. Sure enough, two big, red hook-and-ladder engines barrelled up the street.

The front door creaked open, and Mom came into the living room. Tears trickled down her cheeks. Blood stains spread like blooming flowers on her shirt. A few orange leaves had caught in her windblown hair.

"It's time for you to walk to school, Laura." Mom's voice was hiccupy, as if she was finding it hard to catch her breath.

"June already went by with her mom. I'll go with you. Hurry and change into your tunic."

When I was ready, Mom put Frankie in his carriage and we went outside. I held Marjorie's hand. As we made our way down the front walk, a bright light flashed. A man with a camera around his neck was standing beside the Withers' caragana hedge.

Men in white uniforms lifted a stretcher with Mrs. Withers on it into one ambulance. They put Ronnie in a second one.

"Will they be okay, Mom?" my voice squeaked.

"I don't know, Laura." Mom walked so fast I had to run to keep up. I was late for school, but I still got there on time to recite "In Flanders Fields."

When June and I went home later, the wrecked car was gone from the yard next door.

"Look at that gigantic hole in the house, June. You can see straight into the Withers' living room." I pointed to a large photograph of a man in an army uniform on the piano.

"That must be Mr. Withers," June said. "He's handsome."

Another photograph sat right beside it, one of Ronnie when he was a little boy.

"Do you see his goofy smile?" I asked June. "His two front teeth are missing, but he looks all bright and happy."

Mom was standing in the hallway when I walked through the front door. Her shoulders slumped. She clutched a soggy handkerchief in her hand. "I phoned the hospital just now," she said. "The doctors aren't sure yet whether Mrs. Withers and Ronnie will get better."

I gave Mom a hug. "June is coming over to play."

"You'd better go and change out of your tunic before she gets here."

I grabbed the stairway railing ready to head upstairs but turned first and looked at Mom. "Why did Ronnie drive the car into their house?"

Mom placed her hand over mine. "Ronnie had a sickness that made him sad, Laura. He didn't really know what he was doing."

"Mom, if really sad stuff happens to you when you are just a kid . . . can it make you kind of sad for your whole life?"

"I think sometimes it can, Laura."

ON SATURDAY, Dad sent me to rescue Mrs. Withers' newspaper from its usual place in the caragana hedge. A big photograph of her house with the car in the living room was plastered across the front page of the *Winnipeg Free Press*. In the corner of the photo, you could see our house and Mom, Marjorie, Frankie, and me hurrying down our front walk.

5

Finding Friends

WILL

I FIRST spotted Aneesh last year, on our first day of grade five. He was sitting alone in the cafeteria eating a naan and some curry. A trombone case lay on the floor by his feet. Another musician!

I pushed my glasses up my nose, straightened my shoulders, and went over. "Mind if I sit here?"

"Fine with me," he said.

I pulled out the chair across from him.

"You play trombone?" I pointed to the case on the floor.

"I do. Hoping to get into concert band next year."

"Me too! I play tuba. I'm Will Sanders."

"I'm Aneesh Prasad."

Aneesh was super easy to talk to. As we got to know each other, a tall red-headed girl in a polka dot shirt sitting alone at the end of our table kept staring at us. Halfway through our conversation, Aneesh and I found out we both liked chess.

"Bet I could beat both of you," the redhead said.

And that's how we met Emmaline O'Rourke. It didn't take long for us all to become friends and for Aneesh and me to find out that Emmaline had been *absolutely* right about being able to beat us both at chess.

ON WEDNESDAY at lunch, Aneesh shares some date cookies with Emmaline and me.

"I need your honest opinion," he says with a serious look on his face. "I baked those last night. How'd they turn out?"

I bite into one and give Aneesh a thumbs up.

"There's more where these came from," he tells us. "Want to come over after school and finish them off?"

"I'm so there," Emmaline smiles. Cookie crumbs cling to her braces.

Now's the time, Will, I say to myself. *Tell them the truth about Grandma. Tell them what happened in elementary school—all of it—and why you lied so you don't have to lie again.*

I open my mouth, but my heart starts galloping. My hands are clammy, and they tremble.

I try to take a deep breath, but my chest is so tight I can hardly suck in any air. "S-sorry... I, uh... can't make it. I told Dad I'd meet him, and uhm... pick out a birthday present for Mom."

"What is it with Wednesdays, Will? You always seem to be busy lately." Emmaline sighs.

I bend down and retie my sneaker laces. I wonder what they'd say if they knew the truth. I should just tell them. The longer I put it off, the harder it gets.

What a mess!

GRANDMA GAVE me my own key to her apartment, which is pretty cool. It's on a long leather cord that I wear around my neck, tucked inside my shirt so Emmaline and Aneesh won't see it. As I pull out the key and fit it into Grandma's door on my third Wednesday visit, Mendelssohn the basset hound starts barking up a storm in the apartment across the hall.

"William, I'm in here," Grandma calls.

I follow her voice to the study. She sits at her desk with a gazillion books, messy piles of papers, photographs, colored markers, empty coffee cups, and dirty plates scattered around her. Sheesh! How can she even find her laptop in all that mess?

"Sorry, William. I'm writing a new book and time got away from me."

"What's your new book called, Grandma?"

"*Walk Backwards and Sing!*"

My stomach churns and a shiver shoots down my spine. I imagine what Gregory and Grayson would do with a title like that.

Gregory would jab my chest with his fist. *Think* you *can do two things at once, you little dweeb?*

Grayson would put his face right up into mine. *Let's see if you can walk backwards on those toothpick legs of yours, Baby Will.*

"How about I go and make you a snack." Grandma's words interrupt my frightening thoughts.

"Can I make my own?"

"Of course!"

I yank open the fridge and find a pitcher of ice-water with lemon slices floating in it. Nice! I pour two glasses and stick a bag of popcorn into the microwave.

While it pops, I go into Grandma's study and open the suitcase. She looks up from her computer and smiles as I pull out a book with a dark brown cover called *Flint and Feather*. I take it back to the kitchen with me.

"Do I smell popcorn?" Grandma hobbles from her study to the kitchen. She laughs. "I was sitting at that desk so long my legs fell asleep." She picks up one of the glasses of ice water. "Thanks, William. I needed this."

I toss the book with the brown cover on the table and take the popcorn out of the microwave. I shake the kernels into a flowered bowl Grandma once told me was a gift from a friend who lived in Paris.

"I see you've found my book of Emily Pauline Johnson poems, William." Grandma gently strokes the cover.

"Last year in school, I read about her in a graphic novel by David Alexander Robertson. She was this amazing Indigenous poet." I stuff a handful of popcorn in my mouth.

Grandma's eyes go all sparkly. "I can still recite one of her poems by heart. It helped me when I was in a tough situation not long after our family had left Winnipeg and moved to Rocky Creek. My father had a new job there working with a Dr. Calder."

I shove the Paris bowl across the table. "I've sometimes wondered how you ended up living in Rocky Creek, Grandma."

"I was about to start grade three the summer we moved. Mrs. Sharp was my teacher."

"Can you eat popcorn and tell a sixties girl story at the same time, Grandma?" I grin.

Grandma laughs. "Something tells me we are going to find out."

6

My Brother Could Die

LAURA, 1961

BANG! I was jerked from my sleep by a loud explosion. Marjorie bolted straight up in her bed like a puppet yanked from its dreams by a string. A piece of her hair had escaped from the pink foam curler it was wrapped around. She brushed it out of her eyes.

"What was that sound, Laura?" she whispered, as if danger might be lurking right outside our door and she was afraid to make too much noise. "It sounded like a gunshot."

"I don't know what it was. It can't have been Dad's gun." Mom had made Dad stow his hunting rifle in the barn at Uncle Herman's after he almost shot our brother Frankie last October.

Dad had just returned from a deer-hunting trip with Dr. Calder and had laid the gun down on the passenger seat of our Envoy but forgot to put the safety catch on. When he banged the driver's side door shut, a bullet shot out through the other door. It just missed Frankie, who was playing in the front yard. There was a jagged hole in the Envoy and the bullet was still lodged in the trunk of the big pine.

The loud bang must've woken Frankie up, too, because he wailed, just like he had the day Dad almost killed him. I heard Mom walking up to his room from her bedroom on the main floor, her footsteps playing a familiar creaky tune on the stairs.

A minute later she poked her head around our door holding a rosy-cheeked Frankie in one arm and two blankets in the other.

"The electricity just went off, girls. There's a blizzard out there, and heavy snow brought down the power lines. That was the sound you heard."

Mom put an extra blanket on each of our beds, and the creaking song played backwards on the stairs as she took Frankie to her and Dad's room.

Marjorie and I spread the blankets over the colourful quilts our Grandma Annie had made for us. We snuggled back down, but we couldn't sleep.

"Let's go and see how much snow there is." I wrapped the blanket Mom had just brought around my shoulders and went over to the window. It was all frosted up with a sparkly design that looked like a fairy-tale castle. I used my fingernail to scratch out a little opening. "Oh, my goodness, Marjorie. You've got to see this."

Marjorie jumped out of bed and joined me at the window, scratching her own little peephole through the frost. Our red-and-white Envoy—the one with the bullet hole in the door—was sitting on the driveway completely covered with snow. Only the radio antenna was sticking out. If the streetlights hadn't been lined up in perfect rows marking the edges of the road, you wouldn't have known it was there.

The snow was so high it almost reached the roof of the tiny house across from us. Marjorie and I kept staring at the white world outside till, finally, the chill in the room chased us back into our beds.

"Do you think maybe school will be cancelled today?" Marjorie scratched her nose, then quickly tucked her hand back under the quilt.

"I hope we have school," I said longingly. "I've been memorizing "The Song My Paddle Sings," by Emily Pauline Johnson for the poetry competition at the Rocky Creek Speech Festival. Mrs. Sharp wanted me to recite it in front of the class this morning to practise."

"Aren't you scared?" Marjorie asked. "What if you forget some words?"

"Oh, Marjorie, I could recite that exciting poem in my sleep. Did you know Emily Pauline Johnson was the daughter of a Mohawk Chief? In the poem, she almost drowns."

"That sounds exciting. Can you say the poem for me?"

I launched into "The Song My Paddle Sings." "West wind, blow from your prairie nest . . ."

Marjorie lay on her stomach with her chin cupped in her hands, her eyes glued to my face. I put everything I had into the recitation. When I got to the part where the canoe was going over the rapids, I was so excited I boomed out the line, "Be strong, O paddle! be brave canoe!"

Dad shouted at us from the downstairs bedroom. "Keep the noise down, girls. Go back to sleep."

But just then, there was a noise that was even louder than Dad's voice, louder than my poem recitation, and maybe even louder than the bang that announced the power outage. Someone pounded on our front door so hard I thought it might break.

Marjorie and I jumped out of bed and ran to the top of the stairs just in time to see Dad leave his and Mom's bedroom dressed in his brown bathrobe. The black hair he always kept perfectly combed during the day was a tumbled mess, and his beard was even darker than when he let us rub his scruffy five o'clock shadow after work.

We inched our way down the stairs and stood in the living room as Dad opened the door. A tall man blew into the entryway along with a drift of snow and a blast of icy air. He wore a red-and-black checked wool jacket. His eyelashes were frozen together, and his eyebrows looked like Santa Claus'.

"Doc Johnson," he said, unwinding his scarf to reveal his icicle-laden mustache.

"Is that you, Albert?" Dad asked.

"Yup. My wife, Josie, is the duty nurse over at the hospital tonight, and it's mighty busy. With the phone lines down, she's had no way to reach you. We live close to the hospital, so she sent over one of the orderlies with instructions that I was to get on my snowmobile and pick you up."

"That was kind of you, Albert," Dad said. "Step into the living room where it's warm."

"I'll stay right here if you don't mind, Doc. We need to go."

Dad hurried to his bedroom to change and then got his parka and boots out of the closet and started dressing as Albert talked. "First, I'm taking you to the Fienbergs'. Their eighteen-year-old son Robbie walked to the hospital through the high drifts to let us know his mom was about to give birth to baby number ten. Best if you were at their house when that happens, Doc. I'll wait for you there, because soon as you're done, we need to head over to the hospital. They just admitted a young man with appendicitis. You'll probably need to operate."

Dad pulled on his toque and wound a scarf around his neck. He didn't seem to notice us in the living room, but the man at the door did. "Guess there won't be any school for you kids today. No buses will be able to manage the roads, and the school building will be freezing without the furnace running."

Mom came into the living room and looked at Marjorie and me. "What are you two doing here? Back to bed! It's not even six o'clock. Albert, I wish I could give you a cup of coffee, but of course, I can't plug the perk in."

"No worries, Mrs. Johnson. The generator at the hospital is working and my Josie sent along a Thermos of coffee. Got it out on the snowmobile. Sorry to take your husband away in the middle of a storm."

"Oh, we'll be fine," Mom said. "People don't stop needing a doctor just because there is a blizzard. Do you have any idea when the power will be back on?"

"Could take quite a while with so many lines down. The roads are packed with snow."

Dad put his gloved hand on Mom's shoulder. "I'll get back as soon as I can, Virginia."

The two men went out the front door, slamming it shut behind them. The snowmobile roared to life and then the sound of its engine faded as it headed across the snowdrifts and down the street.

Marjorie and I hadn't moved. Mom smiled at us. "Why don't you two hop into my bed with Frankie and me? We can keep each other warm."

We scurried across the cold linoleum towards our parents' bedroom. When we got to the door, Marjorie shouted, "One... two... three!" and we ran over to the bed and jumped onto the mattress.

Frankie went bouncing up and landed back on the pillows as we flopped down, but he didn't giggle and say *whee!* like he usually did when we sent him flying. I put my arm around him. He felt nice and warm.

I'M NOT sure what time I woke up. Marjorie was snoring on the pillow beside me, but Mom and Frankie were gone.

I crawled out of bed carefully so as not to wake Marjorie. A harsh hacking sound caught my attention, and I followed it to the kitchen where Mom sat at the table holding Frankie. He was coughing so hard that his little body shook. Tears ran from his red-veined eyes and down his rosy cheeks. A big bubble of snot ballooned from his left nostril.

"What's wrong? Is Frankie sick?" I asked.

"Yes. He has croup again." Mom's forehead wrinkled with worry.

"The last time, you put hot water in the tub and closed the door to make the bathroom steamy."

"I know, but the hot water heater uses electricity. With the power off, there is no hot water."

"Could we heat some on the stove . . . oh. No. The stove uses electricity. What are we going to do?"

"I don't know, Laura. Frankie's throat is swelling. I can feel it. I'm worried he soon won't be able to breathe."

"We need to get Dad."

"But how? The phones don't work. I can't leave you children alone and walk to the hospital, even if I could get through all that snow. What if Frankie stopped breathing and you girls were here alone with him?"

I peered out the window. I knew what I had to do even though the thought of it made me dizzy. A wave of fear almost suffocated me. "It's not snowing so hard now. I could go. The sun is up. I could walk to the hospital and get Dad."

"Oh no, Laura. I'd be worried sick. I'm sure the sidewalks haven't been cleared and there could be downed power lines on the streets."

"I'd be careful."

"But it's so cold. The thermometer outside the window says it is thirty-five below."

"I could bundle up. If I get too cold or lose my way, I'll just knock on someone's door and ask for help."

Frankie was coughing so hard I thought he might come apart at the seams. Mom felt his throat and rubbed some more Vicks VapoRub on it from the jar on the table. "I hate for you to have to do this, Laura."

"Do what?" Marjorie came into the kitchen.

"Frankie is sick," Mom replied. "I think Laura may to have to walk to the hospital to get your father."

Marjorie was quiet. Her lip quivered. The only sound in the room was Frankie's raggedy breathing between coughs that seemed to grow worse by the minute.

When Mom started issuing orders, I knew she had decided to let me go. "Marjorie bring your sister some orange juice and a sweet roll for a quick breakfast. Laura, go up to your room and get dressed in layers. Stockings, long underwear and pants, a T-shirt, blouse, and sweatshirt."

When I came back downstairs, Mom had laid out my parka and ski pants, a long red and white scarf she'd knitted for Marjorie last winter, my big leather mittens, and hand-me-down boots from my cousin Fern.

By the time I was ready, I felt like a stuffed teddy bear. My legs had so many layers of clothing, they brushed together with each step. There was only a little slit between the bottom of my toque and the top of my scarf.

Mom planted a kiss right there before sending me out the front door. "I'll be thinking of you every step of the way, Laura."

I walked outside. Marjorie stood at the living room window. Her eyes looked big and scared. I waved at her and fell back onto the snow, making an angel with my arms. When I got up, she was clapping her hands.

As I headed down the street, my feet sank into the snow almost up to my knees. It was hard to lift my legs to move forward. I decided it might be easier to crawl on all fours and I tried that. Amazing! I didn't sink. I kept crawling across the high drifts. I had six blocks to go till I reached the hospital. I turned the corner onto First Street and looked over at the Garber house. The seven Garber children were crowded up to the window. They waved furiously at me. I waved back.

I kept crawling. Another long block stretched ahead of me. I started counting to take my mind off how far I still needed to go. But I got mixed up after a thousand. That's when I had the idea to recite "The Song My Paddle Sings." I started with the first line, and when I got to the last line, I realized I'd reached the end of a block.

When I crawled around the corner, I heard a bark. I looked up and saw something moving in the distance. A black dog—and it was coming towards me! My knees tingled with fear and my heart raced. I had been petrified of dogs ever since one had wandered onto Uncle Herman's farmyard and tried to bite me when I was only five. I forced myself to keep crawling and started reciting my poem again to stay calm.

As the dog approached, I could make out a glossy coat and pointy ears. I couldn't see the expression on its face because it was sniffing the snow as if it were looking for something.

The dog crept closer, growling. I bravely shouted the lines of "The Song My Paddle Sings": "Reel, reel, On your trembling keel ..."

About a metre away, the dog stopped. It snarled.

I kept reciting. "But never a fear my craft will feel."

The dog stopped growling. It tilted its head sideways and sniffed my snowsuit. Then it raced away.

Maybe it thought I was just another dog because I was on all fours. I trembled in relief.

As I started down the next block, a snowmobile rumbled in the distance. I stood up and waved my arms at the driver. Maybe I could get a ride the rest of the way to the hospital. The snowmobile sped toward me.

It was Albert.

He stopped and shouted over the roaring engine, "Laura, what are doing here?"

"My brother Frankie is sick," I yelled. "I need my father."

Albert motioned to the seat behind him and I clambered on and grabbed his waist. I buried my head into his jacket as he guided the snowmobile over the drifts.

When Albert and I walked through the hospital doors, who should be there but Dad. He was talking with a nurse at the front desk.

When he looked up and saw me, his mouth dropped open. "Laura! What's going on?"

Albert piped up. "Found her walking through the snow, Doc. Said her little brother needed help. She was headed for the hospital to find you."

I told Dad about Frankie in a gush of words that tripped over my tongue. Dad gave me a big hug when I was done, and I could feel the stethoscope around his neck bumping against my heart.

"Laura, you'll have to wait here at the hospital while Albert takes me home on the snowmobile to help Frankie."

After Dad and Albert left, the nurse at the front desk noticed me shivering. "Let's get you some hot chocolate, Laura."

She came back with a steaming cup and some hospital blankets, which she wound around me so tightly I felt like an Egyptian mummy.

Albert came to pick me up about a half hour later. "Don't you worry now, Laura. As soon as your dad gave your brother that needle filled with medicine, he started to perk right up. You saved his life, little girl."

I was so happy to hear Frankie was okay that I started to cry.

"There, there now," said Albert patting my head. "I'll be taking you right home."

Later that night, when Mom was tucking Marjorie and me into bed, the lights came back on.

Mom blew out the candle flickering on our nightstand and sat back down on my quilt.

"I'm so proud of you, Laura. You did such a grown-up thing today." Mom tucked in the edges of my sheet.

"Weren't you scared walking in all that snow?" Marjorie asked.

"I was scared, but then I got the idea to recite 'The Song My Paddle Sings,' my poem for the speech festival, and it took my mind off things."

"Can you recite it for me?" Mom asked. "I'd love to hear it."

I started, but by the time I got to part where the rapids were boiling and bounding, my eyelids felt terribly heavy. My voice drifted off just as the spray from the paddle was falling in tinkling tunes away. Mom planted a good-night kiss on my forehead. That's the last thing I remembered.

7

Another Lie

WILL

ANEESH INVITES Emmaline and me over for dinner on Saturday night. When we walk into the dining room, we see that Aneesh's three older brothers have invited friends too. The air vibrates with talking and laughter.

The table looks full, but Aneesh's dad grins widely as he adds extra chairs and directs everyone to move closer together. "Always room for a few more," he says.

Aneesh's mom serves chicken masala and samosas for supper. I lose count of how many samosas I eat.

"Thank you, Mrs. Prasad. That was delicious." Aneesh's mom beams as I push back my chair from the table.

After dinner, Aneesh, Emmaline, and I hang out in Aneesh's room. They're keen to show me the Second World War social studies project they've been working on.

"These are amazing, Emmaline!" I point to all the colourful charts and graphs she's designed to illustrate their research.

"Did you know 45,000 Canadian men and women died doing military service in that war?" Aneesh asks.

I almost blurt out, *My grandma used to live next door to the family of one of those men*, but I stop myself just in time, and swallow hard. If I start talking about Grandma, who knows what I might say?

Emmaline gives me a worried glance. "Are you okay, Will? You look a little pale."

"I'm fine."

"We're doing a bike tour around the city next Wednesday to take photos of a bunch of Second World War statues," Aneesh says. "We thought it would make our project more personal."

Emmaline looks at me. "It would be great if you came along so we could get some good shots of the two of us. It would be way better than just taking selfies."

My chest tightens and I look down at my hands. "I really just . . . have to work on my own project. I'm worried I won't get it done."

"But you took it to school already a while ago. I thought it was finished." Emmaline looks confused.

"I . . . Mrs. Ramos thought I needed to . . . you know . . . add a timeline . . ."

"Oh," Aneesh says. "No problem. We want you to get a good project grade too."

SUNDAY IS a slow day at our place. Dad has a tennis tournament, and Mom is getting ready for lectures. I practise my tuba for a couple of hours in the morning. Not long now till tryouts.

In the afternoon, I find "The Song My Paddle Sings" online. Since I have the time, I memorize it.

MENDELSSOHN IS howling across the hall again when I open Grandma's door on Wednesday number four. She's sitting at the kitchen table having a cup of coffee and a piece of cake.

"Mendelssohn sounds sad," I say.

Grandma wraps her hands around her cup. "He's probably lonely. Leon isn't home. Did I tell you he's a piccolo player for the Winnipeg Symphony Orchestra? They're practising for the upcoming concert season, so he has to leave Mendelssohn alone more than he'd like. I'd offer to have Mendelssohn spend a little time here, but I am so busy trying to finish my latest book. And I'm not really a dog person."

I laughed. "I figured as much after hearing about the dog you met in the snowstorm."

"Would you like some leftover pineapple upside-down cake, William? I made it when my brothers Frank and Peter visited last night."

I nod. Grandma cuts me a generous piece.

When I've polished off the cake, I launch into the opening lines of "The Song My Paddle Sings": "West wind, blow from your prairie nest..."

Grandma's jaw drops, but then she joins in and after a couple of lines, we start moving our arms as if we're paddling down the river. About halfway through the poem, Grandma pulls me off my chair so we can dance around the room while we recite. Our voices get louder and louder. We are shouting when we get to the part about the rapids. "Dash, dash, With a mighty crash, They seethe and boil and bound and splash!"

When the poem is over, I laugh till my stomach aches. I realize that the whole time we were reciting it, I didn't think once about my problems with Aneesh and Emmaline.

After Grandma catches her breath, she says, "Why don't you check the story suitcase for something about a dog?"

I open the suitcase and dig around until I find a newspaper ad with a photo of a dog and a notice for the owner to contact Dr. William Johnson.

"Did you have pets when you were a kid?" I ask when I put the newspaper clipping down on the kitchen table.

Grandma taps the picture. "We had that dog for a week. When nobody claimed it, we took it to a farm, where it lived a long and happy life."

"I'm guessing you have another sixties girl story to tell."

"I do! This one happened when I was in grade four at Rocky Creek Elementary School. It was October 1962, when Russia and the United States were competing to be the most powerful country in the world. They were threatening to use missiles and we thought one might land on us."

"You were worried about missiles in Rocky Creek?'

"Oh yes. Everyone in Canada was worried."

8

Missile Drill

LAURA, 1962

LIKE MOST kids, I was used to regular rehearsals for missile attacks, but that didn't mean I wasn't terrified. We'd heard about missiles all autumn. Whenever we were at school and the town siren rang through the streets of Rocky Creek, we kids had to duck under our desks and cover our heads. I wondered how ducking and covering would keep us safe if a missile ripped through town.

Miss Nelson, our school principal, and our teachers kept telling us not to worry. Probably an attack would never happen. But last night, I'd overheard Mom and Dad whispering to each other about the Russians after I'd gone to bed. They were talking about a place called Cuba. They sounded really scared.

This morning, Miss Davis, our teacher, made an announcement. "When the town siren sounds today, we are not only going to duck and cover. We are also going to practise the walking-home plan that Miss Nelson, explained to you in assembly last week. In case of a missile attack you need to get home to your parents as quickly and safely as possible."

We were working on writing the letter *q* in our penmanship notebooks when the warning blared. My fingers shook as I drained the ink from my fountain pen back into its glass well and hunkered down under my desk.

A minute later, Miss Nelson threw open the door of our classroom and stuck her white head inside. She pointed a shaky finger at us and spit out her order.

"Time to head home, students. Leave now!"

I went straight to the grade two room to pick up Marjorie and a girl named Mattie. In case of a missile attack the fourth, fifth, and sixth graders had each been assigned to one or two younger students. It was our job to make sure they got home safely.

I groaned when they told me I was in charge of Mattie. Why did she have to live near our house? She was the worst kid at Rocky Creek Elementary, so badly behaved that she'd earned the nickname "Bratty Mattie."

Last week she'd gotten in trouble for emptying her lunch box into the garbage can. Wasting food was high on Miss Nelson's list of sins. She had no sympathy when Mattie screamed, "But I hate Spam sandwiches and crab apples!"

A couple of days later, Mattie got sent home for cutting her hair during assembly. "But I wanted a flip like the other girls," Mattie sobbed as Miss Nelson dragged her off by the earlobe.

At the end of the week, the whole school watched Mattie being pushed into the back seat of Constable Steadman's car after she stole a yo-yo from the salesman who'd done a demonstration on the baseball field. I felt sorry for her as she tearfully explained herself to the constable. "But I didn't have money for a yo-yo."

And now it was my job to get Mattie home before a Russian missile sent us off to heaven in a flash of light.

I tried to obey Miss Nelson's instructions to walk home as quickly as possible, but walking quickly wasn't something you could do with Mattie in tow.

"I'm stepping on my shoelaces," Mattie announced as we were about to leave the school yard. "Could you tie them in double knots for me, please, Laura?"

Mattie constantly ran off to pick up gum wrappers she spotted for a chain she was making. "Isn't this a good one?" she'd say, proudly showing me another grimy wrapper before stuffing it into her pocket.

As we passed the town cemetery, Mattie jumped over the fence and did cartwheels across the graves. Talk about ruining her chances of going to heaven if that missile landed on us!

Marjorie waited patiently through all of Mattie's antics but kept sighing in exasperation. I sent her ahead on home.

"Tell Mom I'm on my way," I said.

Mattie spotted the mutt first. He lay whimpering on the boulevard just past the graveyard. A gash on his leg leaked blood onto the sidewalk.

"He must have been hit by a car!" Mattie dropped to her knees and spread her stained orange sweater over the shivering fellow.

The dog was sleek and black with pointy ears and a long tail. He looked like the dog I'd met in a snowstorm last year. I was usually scared of dogs, but this one seemed too weak to be dangerous.

Mattie started to cry, and I couldn't get her to quit. "We have to do something, Laura. We can't just leave him here." She wiped a bubble of snot away from her nose with her sleeve.

"Mattie," I said, "we have to go. The dog's owner will come looking for him. I'm sure."

The mutt whimpered, and little Mattie slid her arms under him. She tried to lift him and staggered backwards.

"Give him to me." I put the injured dog across my shoulders, and Mattie and I started walking. Blood from the dog's leg trickled down my white blouse. I stepped carefully, adjusting to the added weight across my shoulders.

Helping the dog was clearly important to Mattie. She walked the next three blocks to her house quickly.

I went up to the front door with her. She twisted the knob and tiptoed inside.

A scowling woman came out of the kitchen with a toddler hanging onto each leg. She was holding a mixing bowl on her right hip with a wooden spoon in it. "What are you doing home early?" she snapped.

Mattie was silent in the face of her mother's irritation.

"And who's this?" Her mother looked directly at me.

"I'm Laura. I live just a couple of blocks away."

"Well, what are you doing here?"

I explained in rush about the missile drill and how I'd been assigned to get Mattie home.

"My Mattie don't need help getting home. She's no baby. You go on now, Laura. Don't want nobody sticking their nose into our house or our business. And get that dog out of here. He's bleeding all over my floor."

"Aw, Ma. Can't we keep the dog?" Mattie begged.

Her mother laughed harshly. "I've got troubles enough feeding the three of you. Don't need another mouth."

Mattie's mother moved towards me waving her wooden spoon. I turned and fled, nearly tripping and falling as I tried to get off the yard as quickly as possible. It wasn't exactly easy with the dog on my shoulders. He seemed to get heavier with every step.

When I got home, Mom helped me bandage the dog's leg. The fellow was clearly worn out and spent the evening snoozing. He lay under the piano bench while Mom played some of her favourite tunes for us, and then he sprawled over Frankie's feet while he and Marjorie listened to Dad read another chapter from *The Bobbsey Twins*.

I wondered if Mattie's parents ever read to her.

Dad said he would put a notice in the newspaper about the lost dog. Maybe someone would claim him. "If no one does, we'll take him out to the Armstrong's farm," Dad said. "They're my patients. I know they'll give him a good home."

Later, we heard on the radio the possible missile attack had been stopped by an agreement between Mr. Khrushchev, the Russian president, and Mr. Kennedy, the American president.

When Mom tucked me into bed that night, she gave me an extra-long hug. I told her I wanted to invite Mattie over after school to play soon.

"But she's so much younger than you."

"I know, but she might have fun with Marjorie and Frankie. I think she needs a friend."

9

"With a Little Help from My Friends"

WILL

"WILL SANDERS is the best goalkeeper in Winnipeg!" Emmaline screams.

Aneesh bellows through his megaphone. "Way to snag that ball, Will!"

I have an indoor soccer match at the community centre on Saturday night. Aneesh and Emmaline love coming to my games. They cheer me on, loud and proud, from the stands.

There was a time when I thought I'd never play soccer again. In grade four, all the kids on my school team harassed me. After they watched Gregory and Grayson tease me, they joined in. That hurt a lot because my soccer buddies were the friends I thought I could count on, the kids I figured really liked me because I was the best goalie around.

They'd trip me on purpose, hide my gear, put salt in my water bottle, and a bunch of other stuff. It was so bad

I decided I wasn't going to play soccer again. But when we moved to our new house, I saw a poster at the mall about a community soccer team. I thought it might be okay to play somewhere no one knew me. And it was.

In the second period, I deflect a sneaky shot from the other team's striker, and Emmaline yells, "No one can get by you, Will!"

After our win, Aneesh and Emmaline give me high fives. "You're like an octopus out there," Aneesh says. "It's as if you have eight arms and legs waving everywhere and stopping the ball."

All that cheering from my friends feels so good that it almost makes me forget the horrible situation I've gotten myself into. When Grandma lived so far away in Rocky Creek, I never thought my friends would meet her. But now, who knows? What if she had decided to come to my soccer game tonight?

I wipe my clammy hands on my shorts.

WHEN I walk into Grandma's apartment the following Wednesday, I find a note on the fridge: *On a Zoom call in my study. Ice cream bars in the freezer.*

I inhale a bar and then plunk down on the living room couch. This is my fifth Wednesday with Grandma. I have to admit, I like coming here, but it sure has made things complicated with Emmaline and Aneesh. My chest twinges and I sigh.

On a shelf by the TV, there's this really funny photo of Grandpa. I pick it up so I can look at it more closely. His Blue

Jays baseball cap is turned sideways, and he's rolling his eyes. He pulls his mouth into a gigantic grin with his pinky fingers.

I smile. That was Grandpa. Always doing goofy stuff. Always making us laugh. I could use a little of Grandpa's joking around right now. Tears burn my eyes, and I'm wiping them away with the back of my hand when Grandma comes out of her study. She takes one look at my face and puts an arm around my shoulder. She glances at the photo.

"Are you missing Grandpa, William?"

I nod.

"Me too."

"His funeral was the first one I'd ever been to," I tell Grandma.

"I think Grandpa would have loved the way we ended his memorial service by singing his favourite song, 'With a Little Help from My Friends.'"

"Why did he like that song so much?"

"When Grandpa was nineteen, he attended a big music festival in New York called Woodstock. A musician performed 'With a Little Help from My Friends' and your grandpa fell in love with the song."

"Mom plays that song lots, too."

"Your grandpa had so many friends, William. The words of that song are true. We all need friends to help us."

I wipe away another tear, not for Grandpa this time, but because I know I need my friends.

"William, did I ever tell you my grandpa died when I was about your age?"

Grandma pulls down another photo from the shelf, one of a very handsome man in a tailored coat. He's standing on the caboose of a Los Angeles train with a beautifully dressed woman beside him. They look like Hollywood movie stars from the olden days!

"You always had that photo on your mom's old piano in the Rocky Creek house," I say.

Grandma nods. "That's Grandpa Peter and Grandma Annie. They fell in love on a train in 1907 when my grandfather was immigrating to Canada, and many years later they went on a train trip for their honeymoon." Grandma blows some flecks of dust off the photo. "There is a brown leather case that belonged to Grandpa Peter in the story suitcase. It has his initials monogrammed in gold on it. PMS for Peter Martin Schmidt. Why don't you go get it?"

When I return with her grandfather's case, Grandma opens it. Inside there are lots of different compartments filled with interesting stuff.

"Is this jewellery?" I pick up something that looks like a fancy button with a post on the back.

"Those are cufflinks, William. In the 1960s, men held the sleeves of their shirts together with them."

She holds something else up. "This is a tie clip. Grandpa Peter had lots of different ones."

"Did your Grandpa Peter die of a heart attack like Grandpa did?"

"No, he didn't, William. Let's sit down and I'll tell you about it."

10

Where Were You?

LAURA, 1963

THE KIDS in my grade five class at Rocky Creek Elementary School were spread out across the floor painting plaster of Paris maps of Canada. I dipped my brush into the bright orange paint I'd chosen for Alberta. It looked perfect beside the deep green my friend Annemarie was spreading across British Columbia.

There was a knock on the door. Our teacher, Mr. Klassen, said, "Come in."

Arlene Barnes poked her head into our room. Her glossy brown ringlets bobbed as she moved her head from side to side. Her voice was so loud she might as well have been holding a bullhorn to her lips. "President Kennedy's been shot. Principal Nelson says to turn on the radio."

I froze. I looked down as orange paint dripped onto Alberta from my brush, suspended in mid-air.

The door banged shut. Arlene's black Mary Jane shoes clacked down the wooden hallway floor as she hurried to the sixth grade class.

I took a few shaky breaths. Could Arlene's news be true? I had just cut some pictures of the president's children out of the new *Life* magazine yesterday. I had carefully pasted them into one of my scrapbooks.

"Grade fives, let's return to our seats." Mr. Klassen fiddled with the radio dial.

We all sat straight and tall in our desks, our hands folded, fingers interlaced. Everything seemed strangely out of order. It was Friday, and the only thing we *ever* listened to on the radio was our music lesson broadcast on Tuesdays. A lady talked to us in melodious tones about the *do re mi* of the musical scale and taught us songs like "Land of the Silver Birch."

It wasn't long before Mr. Klassen had tuned in CBC.

A man spoke in a deep, serious voice. "John Fitzgerald Kennedy, the thirty-fifth president of the United States of America, was shot as he rode through the streets of Dallas early this afternoon. Within the hour he was dead. Two-hundred-fifty thousand Texans were lining the route of the Kennedy motorcade when, shortly after 12:30, three shots were heard, and the president fell back, blood spurting from his head."

Everyone gasped, almost in unison. Mr. Klassen turned off the radio. I stared at the Neilson Chocolate Bar map of Canada on the wall as if it were a television screen. My friend Annemarie started crying softly. I bit my lip and looked down at my desk. If I looked at Annemarie, I might start crying too.

Mr. Klassen stood at the front of the classroom clasping and unclasping his hands. "This is a very sad day, and we—"

Rrrrrrring! The bell interrupted him.

"We'll return to this after recess." Mr. Klassen dismissed us.

We streamed towards the coatroom and got dressed to go outside. It was cold and windy, so Annemarie and I huddled against the back wall of the school with a bunch of other girls to keep warm.

Annemarie was still crying. "I just saw President and Mrs. Kennedy on the news last night," she said in dramatic tones. "Such a gorgeous couple."

Bertha sniffed. "I don't know what you are so worked up about, Annemarie. It's not like President Kennedy was the leader of Canada."

"But he's so handsome," I said. "Prime Minister Pearson reminds me of a chipmunk with those chubby cheeks of his. President Kennedy looks like a movie star."

Bertha was blowing on her gloves to keep her hands warm, but she stopped to correct me. "You mean *looked* like a movie star, Laura. He is dead, you know."

"Well, pardon me." I glared at Bertha.

The bell rang and we headed back inside. Mr. Klassen was waiting for me at the classroom doorway, a concerned look on his face.

"Don't take off your things, Laura. Your father's receptionist called the school and asked that you go home straight away. Some kind of family emergency."

For a moment, I froze, just like I had when I learned President Kennedy had been shot. My voice stuttered. "Did she say what's happened?"

"No, she didn't, Laura. I hope everything is all right."

I flew out the school's front door and down the street. My worry raced ahead of my feet. Could something be wrong with my new baby brother, Sweet Pete, or with Mom? If something terrible could happen to President Kennedy maybe something terrible had happened to them too.

I heard footsteps behind me and turned around. Marjorie and Frank were running to catch up with me. They must have received the same message I had.

I reached our front door and yanked it open. Sweet Pete was asleep in his cradle in the living room, but Mom was sitting on the hallway floor under the telephone, her back curved away from the wall. The receiver dangled beside her, bouncing up and down on the curly cord. Mom's legs were pulled tight to her body, her arms wrapped around them. Her head rested on her knees. She shook with sobs.

I was really frightened! Marjorie and Frank came up behind me, panting like a pair of scared puppies.

"Should we say something to Mom?" Marjorie wondered.

"Should we hang up the phone?" Frank asked.

"Mom," I said as softly as I could. "Mom."

She didn't look up.

Tires crunched on the gravel driveway and a car door slammed. Dad burst into the house. He stopped, looked at Mom, and then walked slowly towards her. He picked up the dangling receiver, put it to his ear, and then gently rested it back in its cradle. He slid down beside Mom on the floor and put his arm around her shoulders.

"I'm so sorry, Virginia."

Dad beckoned us forward. We floated across the floor like ghosts and sat down. Mom took Dad's hand, and then we all joined our hands together to make a family circle.

"Don't be scared, children," Mom said, finally looking up.

"What's happened?" I ask.

"Grandpa Peter and Grandma Annie..." Dad swallowed hard. "They were on a holiday in Calgary. They were crossing the street and were hit by a car. Grandpa Peter died, and Grandma Annie broke her hip."

We sat in the circle for a long while after that, just holding onto each other. Frank broke the silence with a whisper. "I liked it when Grandpa Peter let me open the leather case with his gold initials on it and pick out which cufflinks he would wear."

I added softly, "He taught me to ride my bike the last time he visited."

Marjorie spoke, hushed and hiccupy. "He was a good whistler."

Mom said, "I'm so glad he knew we named the baby 'Peter' after him." She started to whistle in a breathy kind of way.

Dad murmured, "That was his favourite song, 'Keep on the Sunny Side.'"

Everything was topsy-turvy for days after that. People came and went, bringing food, cards, and flowers. Dad flew to Calgary because they wouldn't let Grandma on the plane with Grandpa Peter's body unless a doctor came along because of her broken hip. Then Dad came home to Rocky Creek, and the whole family piled into the car for the eight-hour drive to Drake, Saskatchewan. We arrived just in time for Grandpa's funeral in the tiny white church he had attended.

It was filled to overflowing. The bench I sat on shook when they sang Grandpa's favourite hymns. The minister talked about how Grandpa's family had immigrated to Saskatchewan from Kansas when Grandpa was just a boy. He described how brave and resourceful Grandpa had been when he had become separated from his family on that journey. The minister said Grandpa had been brave his whole life, always ready to try new things and meet new people.

Everyone was crying, including me, when they lowered Grandpa's coffin into the frozen ground at the cemetery. We passed a shovel along the line so each family member could scoop up a piece of the cold, hard earth to throw in Grandpa's grave. There was a loud thud as each shovelful landed on the coffin.

After that, all my cousins and their parents crowded into my Aunt Eudora and Uncle Herman's farmhouse for a meal. We kids had a giant snowball fight in the backyard later, but our mothers weren't even mad when we come in sopping with snow, our cheeks almost frostbitten.

In the 1960s, people always asked, "Do you remember what you were doing the day President Kennedy was shot?"

If I was being honest, I would have said, "What I remember most about that day is sitting on the floor of our house holding hands with my family and whispering stories about my grandfather." Instead I usually said, "I was in my grade five classroom painting Alberta orange on a map of Canada."

11

A Walk in the Park

WILL

"WHAT SONG is that?"

I look up from my tuba to see Emmaline poking her head into the music room.

"It's a piece I thought I might play for my audition," I say. "It's called 'With a Little Help from My Friends.' It's an old sixties song my Grandpa liked."

"Sounds cool." Emmaline smiles. "When you didn't come to the cafeteria, I thought you might be in here practising."

I didn't go to the cafeteria because every time I look at Emmaline and Aneesh these days I feel guilty about lying to them. "Thanks for checking up on me, Emmaline."

"By the way, Mom says she misses you and wondered if you'd like to come by after school. She's making shortbread."

"But it's Wednesday, and I—"

"Don't bother coming up with an excuse, Will. For some mysterious reason, you are always busy on Wednesdays. What's up with that?"

"I—"

"And one last thing. I know you're nervous about the concert band tryouts. But I'm not. You're going to get in. Trust me." Emmaline closes the music room door.

Trust me, Emmaline said. If I trusted her and Aneesh, I wouldn't keep lying to them.

My grandmother was such a brave kid to face missile scares, walk through a snowstorm, and deal with difficult teachers. If I inherited some of her courage genes, I need to find them now.

I GET a huge surprise when I open the door to Grandma's apartment on Wednesday number six: Mendelssohn is sleeping on her hallway rug. He's snoring like the freight trains that rumble across the bridge just down the street.

On her way to meet me at the door, Grandma steps around Mendelssohn like he's a piece of the furniture "Hello, William. Leon begged me to take Mendelssohn for a few days. He got offered a last-minute gig with the Edmonton Symphony Orchestra. He tried to book Mendelssohn into a kennel, but they were all full. He looked so desperate I couldn't say no."

Even though Grandma talks softly, Mendelssohn snorts and opens his big brown eyes one at a time. He shuffles over and rubs his wrinkly skin against Grandma's leg.

"For someone who doesn't really like dogs, you sure made friends with Mendelssohn quickly, Grandma."

She chuckles. "I know. He's really easy to get along with. We have to go outside every six hours so he can do his business, and that's right about now. Do you want to come along? We could walk to Stephen Juba Park with him. He likes to watch the Canada geese there, and it's a beautiful day for mid-October."

I keep my jacket on and Grandma pulls her purple quilted vest and red wool hat out of the front closet. She clips on Mendelssohn's leash, and we make our way to the elevator together.

Walking along the lane behind Grandma's building, Mendelssohn stops to sniff each tree and chooses one to do his business. Grandma pulls a plastic glove and bag out of her back pocket. She slips the glove on, scoops up Mendelssohn's turds, drops them into the bag, knots it and tosses it in a nearby trash can.

"Wow, Grandma! I'm impressed! You're an expert at that."

Grandma grins.

As we cross the wooden bridge into the park, she says, "Would you like to take Mendelssohn's leash, William?"

I nod. Grandma transfers the leash to me. Mendelssohn lurches forward.

"He's strong." I say.

"Sure is. Hang on tight."

I'm concentrating so hard on keeping Mendelssohn in line that I don't look up for a second or two. When I finally do, I nearly drop his leash. Emmaline and Aneesh are heading straight for us.

My heart and head go into panic mode. *What are they doing here?*

"Will," they shout and come running to meet us.

"You have a dog," Aneesh says. "When did you get a dog?"

I can't move. I knew this day would come. Now that it has, I'm terrified.

"He is so cute," Emmaline says. "What's his name?"

"Why haven't we met him before?" Aneesh crouches down to scratch behind Mendelssohn's ears.

I can't speak.

Grandma places her hand on my shoulder. "Hi. I'm William's grandmother."

Emmaline and Aneesh exchange a shocked look.

Uh oh.

"You're Will's *grandmother?*" Emmaline asks. She wrinkles her brow.

"I am, and the dog's name is Mendelssohn," Grandma replies. "He belongs to my neighbour. I'm just looking after him for a few days. I was glad William popped in to visit and agreed to help me take him for a walk."

Aneesh looks at Grandma and his shocked expression changes to a puzzled one. "You look familiar," he says, crinkling up his nose.

My voice finally comes back. I push my glasses up my nose and straighten my shoulders. I can't hide the truth any longer. "Grandma is an author. She's written lots of picture books. Her name is Laura Johnson."

"Laura Johnson. Of course!" Emmaline smiles at Grandma. "You wrote *Olivia Is Late*, about the girl whose family makes her late for her hockey game. I loved that book when I was a kid. There's a big picture of you on the back cover."

"And you wrote *Is Something Missing?* about the boy who loses everything." Aneesh laughs. "Our teacher read that book to us so many times when I was in kindergarten." He turns to me, his smile fading. "Will, why didn't you ever tell us you had an author for a grandmother?"

"Grandma," I say, feeling numb all over, "these are my friends, Aneesh Prasad and Emmaline O'Rourke."

"And you know my name now," Grandma says smiling. "Let's sit at that picnic table by the river and get to know each other a bit."

Once we're seated, Aneesh politely starts the conversation. "Will's lucky to have you close by, Mrs. Johnson. Both sets of my grandparents live in India. I've only seen them in person twice since I was born." His voice sounds a little stiff.

"My grandmothers both died," Emmaline says softly, glancing at me. "But I used to go fishing with one of them and make pottery with the other."

"Will and I have been sharing stories lately," Grandma says.

I lick my dry lips. "Grandma has been telling me about when she was a girl in the 1960s. She has this suitcase full of old stuff, and every item in the suitcase has a story that goes with it."

"Could you tell us one of those stories?" Emmaline asks Grandma.

"I'd love to," Grandma replies.

"A story from a professional storyteller. What could be better?" Aneesh says.

My shoulders relax. My friends aren't going expose my lie to Grandma, even though they must be wondering why I let them think she was dead.

Grandma turns to me. "William, have you spotted anything else in the suitcase you want to hear a story about?"

"I have been kind of curious about that notebook covered in birch bark."

"Ah," Grandma says. "I wrote stories in that book every summer. My extended family always rented a cottage at Windward Lake for a couple of weeks. My mother had three sisters and one brother, Herman, and they all came with their partners and children.

"We cousins had so much fun skinny dipping at midnight, eating live minnows, building rafts, and having campfires. I covered a small notebook with birch bark that had fallen from the trees growing around the cottage. Just before I'd go to sleep every night, I'd tiptoe around all my cousins spread out across the floor of the cottage in their sleeping bags. I'd head out onto the porch with my flashlight to write in my journal about our day. It was during those summers at Windward Lake that I first started thinking I might become a writer."

12

Lullaby
for a Deer

LAURA, 1964

"HOW MANY frogs have you got in there anyway, Bennie?"
My brother Frank peered into a pail on the blue-and-white
striped dock.

"Twenty-four or twenty-five." Bennie shrugged, as if
catching that many frogs was no big deal.

Nine of us cousins were gathered on the dock of the
cottage my Schmidt side of the family rented at Windward
Lake every year. Carlotta and Fern sat cross-legged reading
Nancy Drew books. Marjorie and I were playing Chinese
checkers with our cousin Bobby. Hubbard and Lillian had
just come back from a long swim and were pulling leeches
off each other.

Bennie surprised us all when he suddenly dumped
his pail of frogs into the lake. They propelled themselves

through the water like little green motorboats and hopped into the bullrushes. We were so intent on watching the frogs that we literally jumped when a long, loud scream pierced the air.

We looked up to see Aunt Peggy rocketing up the path leading from the outhouse to the cottage. Her screaming didn't let up as she charged ahead. She had left the outhouse door banging open in the breeze. She came to a halt in the cottage front yard, her floppy sunhat askew on her brown curls, her pink pedal pushers dragging down around her knees.

"A mouse! A mouse!" The screechy announcement flew from Aunt Peggy's lips, painted their signature fire-engine red. She twirled around like a hula hooper under the towering pine tree beside the verandah.

"I can see her panties," shrieked Bobby in delight. "They're black and lacy!"

"Aunt Peggy, your panties are showing," Bennie shouted.

My aunt looked down. She yelped and wiggled up her pedal pushers. She strode toward the outdoor picnic table beside the big clump of birch trees, where Mom, Grandma, and my other aunts were sipping coffee. My cousins and I followed.

Aunt Peggy was like one of those colour commentators on *Hockey Night in Canada*, sharing stories about our family that repeated on an endless tape recorder loop. The mouse story was about to become part of it.

"I was just answering nature's call and reading the next chapter in *Ship of Fools*, when lo and behold, out of nowhere, this tiny mouse scampered right across my bare feet. I shot up off that outhouse seat as if a snake had bit my behind, jerked up my panties, and the next thing I knew, I was right here in the front yard. Mice give me the heebie jeebies," she concluded, as if we hadn't already figured that out.

The grown-ups smiled, but Carlotta, Aunt Peggy's fourteen-year-old daughter, rolled her eyes. "We are going to hear this story at every family gathering for the next ten years, so let's go swimming or do something. Anything," she begged.

"We could play gin rummy. I brought the deck." I took the stack of faded blue playing cards wrapped in a frayed rubber band out of my shorts' pocket.

"Great idea," Marjorie said. "Uncle Desi just taught us how to play last night, and I don't want to forget the rules."

We go back to the dock where I start dealing out the cards to my sister and four of my cousins.

"I wish Uncle Desi was here to play cards with us this afternoon," Bennie said.

"I do too," I told him. "But I'm looking forward to all the delicious jack the uncles and Dad are going to bring home from their fishing trip to Lake of the Pines. They'll probably be back in time for us to have fresh fish for supper."

Splash!

Now that the Aunt Peggy Show was over, Bobby and Frank had returned to the dock. They were doing cannonball experiments trying to see if they could soak Aunt Nancy, who was stretched out tanning in a lounge chair.

Between dives, Frank picked up Aunt Nancy's birdwatching binoculars and peered out over the water. "A deer," he suddenly exclaimed. "Hey, you guys. I think I see a deer out there right in the middle of the lake."

Bobby grabbed the binoculars from Frank to check things out for himself. "It's just kind of swimming in circles," he reported. "It has a huge rack of antlers."

Aunt Nancy popped up from her beach blanket and took back her binoculars. As she peered through them, the other cousins and I stopped playing gin rummy and strained to see the deer in the lake.

"That deer is in trouble," Aunt Nancy shouted. "He can't find his way back to the shore. We have to help him." She made her way over to the little yellow-and-white boat tied to the dock. Its name, *Ginger*, danced crookedly across the hull.

"Laura and Bennie, you two are the oldest. Hop in the *Ginger* and come with me. Put on your life jackets."

"I'm coming too!" Aunt Peggy pranced down to the dock still carrying her copy of *Ship of Fools*. Aunt Nancy pursed her lips but didn't say anything.

"I hope Aunt Peggy can sit still and be quiet long enough for us to help that deer," I whispered to Bennie. He winked at me.

Once we were settled on the boat's bench seats, Aunt Nancy gave the motor cord a yank, and it sputtered to life. Grandma, all the aunties, and our cousins had gathered on the dock. They waved and wished us luck as we headed out onto the lake.

Aunt Nancy cut the motor when we were a couple metres from the deer. "Now we're all going to be quiet. Peggy, that means you too. Bennie and Laura, I want you to use the oars and get us closer to the deer. We don't want to scare him."

As Bennie and I paddled, my heart galloped in my chest.

"He's awful big," I whispered to Bennie.

"And awful scared," he whispered back.

"Just look at his eyes," Aunt Peggy said.

I looked right into their dark centres glowing green and wild. Was the deer asking for help? As Bennie and I rowed closer, he tried to swim away from us, but he didn't get far. His movements were slow and clumsy.

"He's so tired," Aunt Nancy said.

"I bet he didn't realize how far it was across the lake." Aunt Peggy's voice hitched. "Poor thing."

"What are we going to do?" I whispered. We were so close to the deer now that we could hear him panting.

"He sounds like my dog after we've gone for a long run," Bennie whispered.

"He sounds like Frank did when he had the croup and his breath rattled in his chest like a broken radiator," I said softly.

"I am going to try and hold onto his antlers," Aunt Peggy whispered. "It's the only thing that makes sense."

"Are you sure, Peggy?" Aunt Nancy didn't sound sure about it at all. "He's ten times your size and—"

"Yes. I'm sure," Aunt Peggy said firmly. "Bennie and Laura, you row us up real close. I'll grab onto his antlers, and then, Nancy, you start up the motor just as low and slow as it goes, and we will see if we can tow him to shore."

Bennie and I started to row, and to our surprise, Auntie Peggy began singing softly. "Schlaf, Kindlein, Schlaf." It was an old German lullaby our Grandma Annie often sang to us.

The deer turned towards Aunt Peggy as she started singing. She looked right back at him, holding his gaze all steady and sure. As she sang, her *Ship of Fools* book slid off the seat and into a puddle of water on the floor of the boat, but she didn't even notice.

We were so close to the deer now that I could see the water drops glistening on his brown back. I could smell his wet fur.

Aunt Peggy continued singing and reached out to touch the deer's neck ever so gently. At first it shuddered, but as Aunt Peggy kept singing and increasing the length of her calm strokes, the animal's breath grew more even. Slowly, her hand inched up the deer's neck, and she wrapped her fingers around his antlers.

Aunt Nancy started the motor again on the lowest setting, and the deer shook his head a little but not all wild and angry like I thought he would.

"Laura, sing with me," instructed Aunt Peggy.

As we purred and putted towards the shore, Aunt Peggy and I sang all about the sheep and trees and stars and the mother and father.

"Let's sing along," Aunt Nancy urged Bennie, and they joined in too.

Our voices echoed across the water. The aunts and Grandma and the cousins, who were still standing on the dock, started to sing too, all soft and sweet. We serenaded that deer with our gentle family choir.

As we neared the cottage, the aunties rounded up the cousins and herded them inside. They were worried about what that deer might do when he came out of the water. About a metre or so from shore, the animal found his footing, and Aunt Peggy let go of his antlers. He stumbled up the beach and across the cabin front yard into the woods.

That night, after our jackfish supper was devoured, we played gin rummy with Uncle Desi again. Aunt Peggy had told the deer story twice already. Now she was sitting in the rocking chair reading *Ship of Fools*, its pages all curled up from its time in the water at the bottom of the boat.

I watched her for a minute and shook my head. How could this aunt, who was terrified of a little mouse, stay so calm when she had to help a huge, frightened deer?

I didn't think I'd ever be able to erase the picture in my mind of my aunt holding onto those gigantic antlers and singing a German lullaby to a huge buck. I couldn't believe I was doing it, but I asked, "Could you please tell the deer story one more time, Aunt Peggy?"

13

Alone

WILL

WE ALL stay at the picnic table without saying a word after Grandma finishes telling us about the deer rescue at Windward Lake. Mendelssohn sits quietly as if he's thinking about the story too. He breaks the spell when he barks excitedly at a pair of Canada geese waddling up out of the river.

"That was amazing," Emmaline says. "I felt like I was right there in the boat when you were rescuing the deer."

"I'd like to meet Aunt Peggy," Aneesh grins. "She sounds like fun. I guess she's passed away by now."

"Oh yes," Grandma replies, "though she lived to be nearly a hundred. She told family stories till the day she died."

"Well, *your* family story really brought her alive for me."

"Thanks, Aneesh," Grandma smiles. "Now that we've met each other, please know you and Emmaline are welcome to visit me anytime. William comes to my apartment every Wednesday. I'd love to have you join him."

Emmaline's mouth twitches. She glances at Aneesh, but he turns his head and stares at the river.

I press my lips together and look down at my feet. There's nothing I can say. Now my friends know I've lied about more than Grandma being dead. They know I haven't spent the past few Wednesdays grocery shopping or taking an extra tuba lesson or looking for a birthday gift for Mom or making a timeline for my soccer project.

That familiar tightness grabs my chest again and it hurts to breathe. I feel dizzy.

Aneesh gets up from the picnic table and puts out a hand to shake Grandma's. "It's been so nice to meet you. Thanks for the kind invitation to your home." Aneesh sounds like a robot repeating programmed lines. He scratches Mendelssohn behind the ears. "See you, buddy." Then he follows the path leading out of the park.

Emmaline looks right at Grandma and doesn't even glance my way. "We'd love to hear more of your stories sometime. Thanks for telling us this one." She runs to catch up with Aneesh.

Mendelssohn gives a little yelp, and Emmaline turns back, waving. "Goodbye, Mendelssohn."

My friends leave the park without saying a word to me.

THE NEXT day, Aneesh and Emmaline avoid me completely. They aren't at their lockers on either side of mine when I stow my lunch and coat in the morning. In class, they sit at a table with four other students. We always save spots for each other, but not today. There is no place for me.

I stand in the doorway staring at Aneesh and Emmaline chattering away with the other kids. Finally, Mrs. Ramos, our teacher, puts her hand on my arm and says gently, "Will, there's an empty chair at that table near the window."

At noon, my friends don't show up in the cafeteria, so I eat my pastrami sandwich alone. I can barely finish half of it.

I head to the basketball court after school thinking maybe a miracle will have happened and they will be there. But there are only a bunch of guys planning a pickup game on the court. The bleachers are empty.

ON WEDNESDAY number seven, I hear two lively voices when I enter Grandma's apartment.

I recognize both of them. My heart feels lighter.

"Is that you, William?" Grandma sings out happily. "Come and meet my company."

My great-aunt Marjorie sits at the table with Grandma, and they're playing cards. "My, William, how you've grown!" she exclaims.

"Hi, Aunt Marjorie," I say.

"I've got a particularly good hand here, William, so I'm not going to put it down to give you a hug." Aunt Marjorie grins.

"What are you playing?" I ask.

"Gin rummy," Grandma and Aunt Marjorie say in unison. They laugh.

I smile. "That's the game your Uncle Desi taught you at Windward Lake."

"How do you know that?" Aunt Marjorie looks at Grandma. "Laura, have you been telling this boy stories about our childhood?"

Grandma smiles. "Maybe."

"I hope she hasn't revealed too many secrets." Aunt Marjorie winks.

"Grandma, can I use your computer while you two finish your game? I have to hand in this big social studies project tomorrow and I just need to fill out the rubric online for my teacher."

"Be my guest. I'll call you when I'm ready to serve the fruit and chocolate tray. By the way, William, how are your friends Emmaline and Aneesh?"

My chest tightens. "They're fine," I say.

"It was so lovely to meet them last Wednesday," Grandma continues. "I hope you'll bring them round to see me soon."

"Sure," I say in the most normal tone I can muster.

I take my school bag into Grandma's study and settle into the big swivel chair at her desk, in front of her computer. A folder is open on the screen. It looks like it's full of the stories she's told me. I notice the words "*Seventeen* Magazine" in one title. I think I remember seeing a magazine called *Seventeen* in the suitcase.

Curious, I open the document. I spot the name "Herman" in the first paragraph. He was Grandma's uncle, her mother's brother. She's talked about him lots—why he didn't go to war, the big snowball fight on his farmyard after her grandfather's funeral. Didn't her dad's rifle end up at Uncle Herman's after he almost shot Grandma's brother Frank?

What does Uncle Herman have to do with *Seventeen*?

I keep reading.

14

Seventeen Magazine

LAURA, 1965

MY PARENTS were off to a medical convention in Saskatoon, an annual summer event. Dad went to lectures during the day while Mom shopped and then joined Dad for fancy convention dinners. Frank, Marjorie, Sweet Pete, and I each stayed at the home of a different relative while Mom and Dad were gone. I always went to Uncle Herman and Aunt Eudora's farm.

After we'd arrived, everyone enjoyed strawberry pie and coffee around the kitchen table. Then my Uncle Herman said his good-byes and headed back out to the field. Aunt Eudora and my cousin Fern wished my parents a good trip before they got busy cleaning up our dishes. Grandma Annie and I went out to the car with Mom and Dad to see them off.

"Have a good time, Laura. I love you." Mom gave me a final hug before she slid into the passenger seat.

Dad took my suitcases out of the trunk and got into the driver's seat. He rolled down his window and looked at me square and serious. "Laura, be sure to use your common sense while you're here."

As my parents drove away, Grandma Annie gave me another hug. "I'm so glad you've come, Laura."

One of the things I loved about staying with Uncle Herman and Aunt Eudora was that Grandma Annie lived with them. She had moved in after Grandpa Peter's accident.

Grandma Annie always made my favourite foods while I was at the farm. Last summer, she taught Fern and me how to embroider. We made beautiful handkerchiefs for our parents with their initials in the corners. I wondered what Grandma would teach us this year.

My cousin Fern was twelve just like me. She came bouncing out of the house now. "Let's take your stuff up to my bedroom, Laura." She picked up my suitcase and I grabbed the handle of my Barbie case.

"You brought your Barbies?" Fern's voice rose in a question mark.

"We had so much fun with them last summer," I said.

Fern spoke softly. "We're a bit too old for Barbies now, Laura. I've got some other stuff to do that's way better."

What was she talking about?

When Fern and I came back outside, my seventeen-year-old cousin Lillian was pulling onto the yard in the family's Studebaker. "Welcome back, Laura." She climbed out of the car and gave me a warm smile. "Sorry I missed your parents, but I was doing a little shopping in town."

"There are strawberries left to pick," Aunt Eudora called, coming out of the house and setting a stack of empty syrup pails on the porch. All the women grabbed a pail and headed out to the strawberry patch.

It was dreadfully hot, and my back grew stiff from bending by the time we headed inside, our pails brimming with berries. Aunt Eudora and Grandma Annie got busy in the kitchen making strawberry syrup.

"You girls worked hard," said Aunt Eudora offering us each a glass of ice-cold lemonade and a gingersnap. "If you'd like, you can go and play now."

We raced upstairs to Fern's room, where we shared a high four-poster double bed covered with the Circle of Time quilt Grandma Annie had made. It was full of interesting designs and shapes.

I flopped onto the bed while Fern got down on her knees and pulled a blue travelling case out from under it. The case was a wedding present from Grandpa Peter to Grandma Annie before they made their honeymoon train trip to California.

"Have you ever seen *Seventeen*?" Fern opened the case and handed me some magazines from the stack inside.

"No, I haven't. Do you have to be seventeen to read it?"

"Of course not, silly. They have articles about fashion and boys and stuff."

"Let's go out to the caboose and look at the magazines there."

"Great idea!" Fern put the magazines back in the case and snapped it shut. "You never know when Mom might come up here. I don't want her to find out I have these."

The caboose was a tall wooden box with sleigh runners on the bottom. When Mom was a little girl, her family hitched the caboose to their horses in the winter. Everyone sat on benches inside, except my grandfather, who stood at the open window in the front holding the horses' reins and guiding them over the snowy fields.

Now the caboose sat abandoned near a stand of birch trees. The runners were rusty, and the wood was starting to rot, but it made a perfect hiding place. We plunked down in the doorway.

Fern opened the travelling case and handed me half the magazines. "Here you go."

"Isn't this Rock Hudson?" I pointed to a tall, dark-haired movie star on the front cover of the top magazine. He was on a sailboat, clutching a thick rope and leaning out over the water.

"Of course it's Rock Hudson," Fern said. She pointed to the three girls on the cover with him, wearing pastel shirts and jaunty sailor hats. They gazed up at Rock adoringly. "Look at those cute outfits."

Fern flipped through a few pages and then shoved her magazine into my lap. "What is this about?"

The magazine was opened to a page with a smiling girl wearing a dress covered with buttercups. She sat under a palm tree. She had long dark eyelashes and her blonde hair was pulled back with yellow ribbon. Fern read the words beside the girl in bold print, "Be sunny. Be saucy. Be summer's song. But be sure."

Fern looked up at me and wrinkled her forehead. "Sure of what?"

I spotted the tiny row of blue boxes at the bottom of the page with the word "Kotex" on them. "It's an ad for sanitary napkins."

"What are you talking about?"

"Hasn't your mom told you about getting your period?' I asked.

"*My* period?" Fern scrunched up her nose. "Periods are at the end of sentences!"

"Well . . ." I bent down and pulled up my bobby socks one by one, wondering how to explain. "When you turn a certain age—"

"What's a 'certain age'?" Fern demanded.

"Could be our age," I said, "but when girls reach a certain age, they start getting this thing called a 'period' every month."

"But what is it? Why has no one—"

Whoosh! We felt a gush of air directly above our heads. Looking up, we saw a huge grey bat winging away. Then— *whoosh!*—another bat came sailing out of the caboose door. It flew so close to my ear it ruffled my brown curls.

"Run!" Fern screamed. She shot to her feet, flew from the caboose, and sped into the birch clump ahead.

I jumped up too, sending the *Seventeen* magazines flying. I raced after Fern. We wove our way among the trees until we reached the field behind them. Uncle Herman was at the far end, plowing. He drove right over when he saw us. When he jumped down off the tractor seat, Fern threw her arms around him. "Oh, Dad, it was terrible. There were two bats in the caboose, and they flew out right over our heads."

"Laura, are you alright?" He raised an eyebrow in my direction.

"I'm fine. It's my first time seeing a bat, though."

"Kind of nifty creatures, aren't they?" Uncle Herman smiled reassuringly.

"But Dad, they might have had rabies!" Worry wrinkled Fern's face.

"I doubt that, but I'll walk back to the caboose with you girls and check whether there are any more bats around."

Uncle Herman stopped at the barn to pick up a broom, and we headed towards the caboose. "You young ladies just wait outside while I investigate." Uncle Herman stepped bravely into the caboose brandishing his broom.

He came back out a minute later. "No bats in there," he reported cheerily. "Must have been a pair on their own. Maybe it just got too hot in the caboose so they went to find another place to roost till sunset. And speaking of sunset, you girls better get back to the house to help with supper."

"Yes, Dad," Fern said.

"But first, you might need to do a little picking up around here," he added, calmly surveying Grandma's upside-down travel case and the *Seventeen* magazines littering the ground.

"We will, Dad."

Uncle Herman winked and went back to his tractor.

"Do you think he'll tell your mom about the magazines?" I asked.

Fern shook her head. "He often says he only tells us stuff on a need-to-know basis. I don't think this would be something he'd figure Mom needs to know."

She was right. At supper, Uncle Herman didn't say anything about the magazines, but he told Aunt Eudora and Lillian and Grandma all about our bat adventure. He described how, like a knight in overalls, he had leaped off his tractor steed and charged into the caboose with his trusty broom held high to flush out any bats.

He had us all laughing.

I liked Uncle Herman. He had started teaching me to drive his truck last summer. It was a little scary behind the steering wheel, but Uncle Herman said farm girls needed to learn. Lillian had been able to drive the truck on her own by the time she was twelve.

Other times, Uncle Herman took us target shooting in the far field. That scared and excited me. I was getting pretty good at hitting the tin cans he perched on fence posts for us to aim at. I wasn't totally sure if my parents would approve of me shooting or driving, but I figured I wouldn't say anything about it unless they did.

I had a scary dream that night. Our family was having a picnic in Assiniboine Park. While the rest of us played a game of croquet, a whole flock of bats swooped down, hooked their claws into Sweet Pete, and lifted him from his carriage. They carried him off into the sky. He was screaming.

I screamed too and bolted upright in bed. My heart was beating faster than the time I had crawled over the snow to get help, faster even than when the air raid siren went off and we had to hurry home in case Mr. Khrushchev had sent a missile winging our way.

I glanced over at Fern. I guess I hadn't screamed as loud as I thought. She was still sleeping beside me, her breathing even and sure. I needed to go to the washroom. Lifting the Circle of Time quilt, I swung my legs over the side of the mattress and slid to the floor. I padded barefoot along the cold linoleum to the bathroom. The door creaked as I closed it.

I used the toilet. Just before I flushed, I noticed a trickle of blood in the bowl. I knew right away what was happening. When I was ten and Mom was pregnant with Sweet Pete, she read me and Marjorie a book called *Susie's Babies*. It was about a mother hamster who was pregnant and gave birth. Later, Mom explained what periods were and what would happen when Marjorie and I got them for the first time. She even showed us the Kotex pads we would wear in our panties.

But Mom wasn't here, and I didn't have any Kotex pads. What was I going to do? I couldn't tell Fern. She thought a period only came at the end of a sentence. If I went into Aunt Eudora's room to tell her, I'd wake up Uncle Herman too, and that might be embarrassing. Grandma Annie was getting hard of hearing, and it would be too difficult to explain what had happened without shouting.

Dad had told me to use my common sense. It took a moment to figure it out, but I did. Lillian was seventeen. She would have Kotex pads. I'd talk to her. I tiptoed down to her room, opened her door carefully, and walked over to her bed.

"Lillian," I whispered, shaking her shoulder gently.

She opened her eyes and sat up. "Laura, what are you doing here? Is something wrong?"

Tears welled. My voice sounded hiccupy as I told her what had happened.

Lillian took a Kotex pad out of the bottom drawer of her dresser and an extra pair of panties. She put her arm around my shoulders and guided me down to the bathroom to show me what to do.

When I was all set to rights, she said, "Now don't you worry, Laura. When you need another pad just come into my room and take one from my dresser." She tilted her head. "How did you know you were having your period?"

"Mom told me all about it."

Lillian smiled. "Well, you were lucky. Plenty of girls don't know anything about it. They're terrified when it happens for the first time."

"Thank you for helping me, Lillian."

She gave me a hug. "Don't worry. This is just between you and me. I won't say anything to anyone else."

I whispered good night to Lillian and went back to Fern's room. Moonlight shone through the open window. It lit my way as I crossed the floor and crawled back into bed. I snuggled deep down under the Circle of Time quilt. My last thought before I fell asleep was how excited Mom would be when I told her what had happened.

15

A Walk to the Forks

WILL

"WILL, CAN you stay after class for a moment?" Mrs. Ramos stops me as I'm leaving at the end of the day. When the other kids are gone, we sit down at a couple of student desks.

"Will, I've noticed there seems to be some sort of disagreement going on between you, Emmaline, and Aneesh. The three of you are such good friends."

I look down at my hands. I'm not sure what to say.

"Maintaining friendships can be tough sometimes. If you'd like to talk to me about what's going on, maybe I can help."

My chest tightens. "Thanks Mrs. Ramos. I'm the only one who can fix things."

She puts a hand on my shoulder. "Making things right with friends can be tough. Let me know if I can help in any way."

WHEN I get to Grandma's on Wednesday number eight, piccolo music is seeping out into the hallway. Whatever Leon is playing doesn't match my mood at all. It's way too cheerful.

As soon as the front door clicks closed, Grandma calls from her study. "William, can you come in here for a minute?"

I poke my head around the corner. Grandma is sitting at her desk.

"William, did you happen to read a story called '*Seventeen* Magazine' on my computer when you were here last week?"

"Yes." My cheeks grow warm. "How did you know?"

"Oh, after Marjorie left, I found that story open on my screen."

"I'm sorry, Grandma. I probably should have asked your permission first."

"It's okay. I was going to let you read it one day anyway."

I wasn't expecting Grandma to say that! "So, the story wasn't supposed to be private?"

"Why would it be, William? I know your parents have talked to you about what happens during puberty. A girl getting her period is a perfectly natural thing. Kids shouldn't be embarrassed or shy to talk about it. I just wanted to let you know that if there is anything in that story you ever want to talk to *me* about, you absolutely can."

"Thanks, Grandma."

"Why don't you choose something else from the story suitcase?" she says, pointing at it. "Then let's walk down to the Forks and have a cinnamon bun and hot chocolate at the

Tall Grass Prairie Bakery while we talk. This could be one of the last nice autumn days before it snows."

I can almost smell cinnamon buns and hot chocolate as I dig around in the suitcase. I pull out an old, folded map and open it. There's a route traced in red pen from Rocky Creek, Manitoba, to a place in North Dakota called Wahpeton and then to Montreal.

"Is this map from a family vacation, Grandma?" I ask when we are getting on our hats and jackets in the front hallway.

"Yes, it is. Road trips in the sixties were very different than they are now. Cars weren't air conditioned, and many of them didn't have seatbelts. There was no such thing as Google Maps. We had to rely on folded paper maps to find our way."

Grandma and I head to the elevator and out the front door of her building. As we stroll down to the Forks, she tells her story.

16

Love and War

LAURA, 1967

"LAURA, GET your nose out of that book and look at the beautiful scenery."

If I had a dime for every time Mom had said that to me already on this trip, I'd be able to buy that tube of tawny peach lipstick I've been eyeing at the Rocky Creek Five to a Dollar Store.

"What's that book about anyway?" Frank leaned across Marjorie, who was wedged between us in the back seat of our car. He tried to grab my novel.

"Mom, Frank is kicking me again," Marjorie yelled.

"That's the third time in the last hour, Frank." Dad's eyes stay fixed on the shimmering pavement ahead. "Do I need to stop the car and have a serious talk with you?"

"No, Dad." Frank lifted his sweaty hand from my novel, jerked away from Marjorie, and settled sullenly into his seat, his head turned toward the window.

"We'll stop for lunch in about forty minutes." Mom sighed. She'd been fending off the flying fingers of my little brother Sweet Pete. He was perched between my parents on the fold-down armrest in the front seat and seemed determined to grab the map of North and South Dakota spread out in Mom's lap.

Mom was the navigator on our vacations. Although she liked to think she knew where we were going, we often got lost. It would be a miracle if we reached the Black Hills by tomorrow like we'd planned.

We were on a family trip to Montreal for Expo 67, a world's fair being staged for Canada's 100th birthday. Because Mom had always wanted to visit the Black Hills, we were heading there first.

"William, let's drive to Wahpeton. It isn't too far from a place where my Dad spent some time when he was immigrating to Canada. We'll have lunch there."

"You're the boss, Virginia." Dad always followed Mom's driving instructions even if he wasn't sure they'd get us where we wanted to go.

Mom expertly folded up North and South Dakota and stuck them in the glove compartment where Sweet Pete couldn't get at them.

"I'm going to start praying for rain," Marjorie whispered.

Looking up from my book to check the cloudless sky, I had a feeling my sister's prayers weren't about to be answered. We kids loved it when it rained on a trip. Those were the only times we got to eat at a restaurant. Otherwise, we'd pull in at some picnic spot where meals became long and complicated. Dad had to wrangle the battered blue cooler out of the trunk. Mom would open up a giant can of pork 'n' beans, and add a pack of sliced wieners to it, or make roast beef sandwiches with mustard and wilted lettuce on bread that was slightly damp. Later, she'd heat water on the gassy green Coleman stove, and Marjorie and I had to wash and dry the Melmac picnic dishes.

I went back to my book, *The Mapmaker*, by Sadie Stevenson. I'd found it at the second-hand store when I went shopping with the crisp new one-dollar bill Grandma Annie always tucked into our birthday cards. The book had been a bargain for a quarter.

Thank goodness Frank hadn't gotten a hold of my novel. He would have made fun of all the romance. I'd reached the part where Pedro, the South American cartographer, took a blanket up to the barn hayloft to spend a moonlit night with his new wife. Magnolia was a shy girl from Georgia who was head over heels in love with her dashing groom.

"Please let it rain." Marjorie was still praying, but God wasn't listening. Our new Mercury Marquis was a boat of a car, and Dad steered it into port near a cluster of pine picnic tables in Wahpeton Park. Up ahead, the sun glistened off a gigantic catfish statue. Frank shot out of the car to look at it.

"You girls stretch your legs a bit. I'll make lunch." Mom began taking things out of the cooler. Sweet Pete sat on the ground nearby, happily throwing pinecones at unsuspecting squirrels. Dad stood guard by the picnic table with a fly swatter to chase away insects.

I wandered off with my book and found a huge rock to lean against. I hunkered down to find out how things were going with Pedro and Magnolia. Before I'd even opened *The Mapmaker* to the right spot, I noticed a young man and woman having a serious talk at a picnic table not far from me. The man wore an American military uniform, and his head was shaved. He had jet-black eyebrows. The woman wore a long, flowy skirt, peasant blouse, and big hooped earrings. Her curly brown hair almost touched her waist. Flaming red toenails peeked out of her open-toed sandals.

I felt a pang of jealousy. Mom had said I couldn't paint my nails till I was sixteen.

I opened my novel so it looked like I was reading, but the mapmaker and his new bride couldn't draw my attention away from the real-life story unfolding before me.

"You have to go back, Charles," the woman pleaded softly.

"I'm not going back. They've started shipping guys off to Vietnam. What will you do if that happens to me?'

"I'll be fine, Charles."

"You won't be fine. Not with the baby coming. Not with that angry father you live with. What if he makes you give the baby up for adoption?"

"Ma will help me."

"Your Ma's a fine woman, Sophia. But she doesn't stand a chance with your father around."

"But if you don't go back, they could arrest you."

"We'll go to Canada. Lots of people are doing it. We could leave right from here. Drive your car up to the border and cross at this place called the Northwest Angle. The authorities wouldn't even know."

I was so involved in Charles' and Sophia's story that I didn't notice Marjorie had slipped down beside me till she pulled my hair. "Are you eavesdropping, Laura?" she whispered.

I put my finger to my lips and whispered back, "Be quiet, you nincompoop."

Marjorie sulked for a minute, but soon she was caught up in the conversation too.

"I love you so much, Sophia. You are all I think about when I am away from you."

"I love you too, Charles, but I don't want us to start our life together on the run, scared and always looking over our shoulders."

"Lunch is ready." Mom's voice trilled across the park. Even Charles and Sophia looked her way. Marjorie and I got up and went over to join the rest of the family.

Frank took his first bite of the lunch, let out a long "Mmmmmmm..." and wolfed down his food.

Mom had outdone herself. She'd scrambled eggs on the stove and added bits of ham for Denver sandwiches. We had Old Dutch potato chips and dip too, made with Lipton's onion soup mixed into Miracle Whip mayonnaise.

I started to eat and then glanced back at Sophia and Charles. Sophia had nestled her head between Charles' shoulder and his neck.

"Laura, you've hardly touched a bite," Mom said. "What are you staring at?"

I looked back at Mom.

"Laura, staring isn't polite. Nice girls—"

A loud siren split the air. A black car with an eagle and the words UNITED STATES ARMY on the side pulled into the parking lot. Three men in dark blue uniforms stepped out. They slipped on sunglasses and marched towards Charles and Sophia. Their boots thumped with each step.

The couple jumped up. Charles wore a grim expression but clung to Sophia's hand. She was sobbing.

"Charles Maxwell Merriweather, you are under arrest for being absent from your post without leave," boomed one of the officers. The other two stepped forward. One put Charles' hands behind his back and the other handcuffed them. They took Charles to their car.

"I love you, Sophia," he shouted, twisting his head to look back at her.

"I love you too, Charles," she called out bravely.

Everyone in the park was watching the scene as if it was an episode of *The Fugitive*. After the military car drove away, we all kept looking at Sophia. Even Mom, who had told me not to stare, was staring.

Sophia picked up her purse from the picnic table and walked briskly towards the parking lot. She slipped into a baby blue Volkswagen. As she pulled off onto the highway, Mom said, "Well, that's the most exciting thing I've seen in a while."

"Wasn't it romantic, Laura?" sighed Marjorie.

"Romantic," Dad sniffed. "Seems like those two didn't use their common sense."

As we drove towards the Black Hills that afternoon, Mom didn't need to remind me to get my nose out of my book. I wasn't reading. I was imagining what would happen to Charles and Sophia. I concocted a dozen different endings to their story in my head. I tried to make most of them happy. I wondered if someday a man would love me the way Charles loved Sophia or the way Pedro, the mapmaker in my book, loved Magnolia.

I wondered if Dad had ever felt that romantic about Mom. I looked at him tapping his fingers on the steering wheel and humming an Elvis tune while Mom stroked Sweet Pete's sweaty little head, resting in her lap. Right then, Mom and Dad turned towards each other and smiled. My parents sure didn't look like they belonged in a romantic story, but maybe there were things about them I didn't know.

17

A Costume
That Fits

WILL

GRANDMA'S STORY about Charles and Sophia makes me
curious about the Vietnam War, so I ask Mrs. Ramos about
it on Thursday morning.

"The US involvement in Vietnam was very controversial,"
she says. "Many people supported it at first, but many oth-
ers protested the war. And lots of Americans escaped the
draft by moving to Canada. I once visited the Vietnam Vet-
erans Memorial in Washington, DC. It has nearly 60,000
names of American soldiers who died in that war. You can
look them up online. Of course, the number of Vietnamese
who were killed is much, much higher."

At morning recess, I use the computer lab to Google the
memorial. Then I search for Charles Maxwell Merriweather.
He died in 1968, just a year after Grandma's family saw him
in the Wahpeton park. It wasn't the happy ending Grandma
had hoped for.

I sit alone with my pastrami sandwich by the cafeteria window. It's raining today, so the place is full. There are only three empty seats, and they're all at my table. Just as I take the first bite of my sandwich, Emmaline and Aneesh walk in. They look around the crowded room until they see me and the empty seats.

Aneesh tugs Emmaline's sleeve, as if he wants to walk away. Emmaline shakes her head and marches toward me with Aneesh dragging along behind. She sits right next to me, and Aneesh sits across from her. They start eating.

My hands feel clammy.

Emmaline says, "I heard you talking about the Vietnam War with Mrs. Ramos, Will. Did your grandma tell you a story about it?"

She's talking to me! I nod, my heart thumping too hard to speak.

"What did your Grandma have in the story suitcase to go with it?" Emmaline asks.

"An old road map," I say, my tongue thick.

I glance at Aneesh. He bites into his pizza and stares at the table.

I roll a green grape in my hand. If I try to eat it, it might stick in my throat.

Emmaline folds her arms across her chest. "Will, we want to know what's been going on."

I swallow hard. How do I even begin?

"You let us believe your grandmother was dead and of course we know she's not," Emmaline continues softly.

"Then you lied about where you were on Wednesdays and what you were doing. Why?"

My chest tightens. I wipe my hands on my pants and start slowly. "At my old elementary school, there were these..." I take a deep breath. "There were these bullies."

"What did they do to you?" Aneesh demands.

I grip my chair and try to keep my voice from trembling.

"It... it started with teasing, I guess. You know... about how skinny I was and my curly hair. They called me a loser for liking chess and said only a moron would play a big ugly instrument like the tuba."

"I don't get it. What does that have to do with your grandmother?" Emmaline asks.

I look down. "They... they found out she wrote books for little kids, so they took them out of the library and looked for ways they could use them to tease me. One of her books is called *When a Baby Cries*, so they started calling me 'Crybaby Will.' I'd walk down the hall and kids would chant 'Crybaby Will, Crybaby Will, Crybaby Will'..."

I twist my fingers together. "You know that book of Grandma's you liked, Emmaline, *Olivia is Late?* One lunch hour, they locked me in a closet and yelled through the door, 'You're gonna be late for class, Will, just like Olivia.'"

I glance at Aneesh. "And your favourite book, *Is Something Missing?* Well, they'd steal stuff from my desk and my backpack. And when I'd go looking for it, they'd say, 'Crybaby Will, *is something missing?*'"

Emmaline and Aneesh look at each other and frown.

"That's awful, Will, but I don't get what that has to do with lying to us," Aneesh says.

The cover of *Why Are You Naked?* flashes across my mind, and my pulse starts racing. Sweat drips down my forehead. How do I tell them about that? How can I say out loud what happened later?

"Well?" Aneesh demands.

I can't speak. I can hardly breathe.

"I'm sorry you got bullied, Will," Emmaline says.

The buzzer goes for afternoon classes, and my friends leave.

I ARRIVE at Grandma's on Wednesday number nine with my Harry Potter costume crunched up in my backpack. Halloween is coming soon. Last year, Aneesh, Emmaline, and I went to a Halloween party at the community centre where I play soccer. We dressed up as Superman, Batman, and Wonder Woman. We had a great time! This year we'd decided to be Harry, Ron, and Hermione since I'd borrowed a Harry Potter costume from my cousin Alex when I visited him in Vancouver over the summer.

Maybe Aneesh and Emmaline will come up with new costume ideas now that we aren't a trio anymore. My chest tightens. I have to talk to them again and try to fix things by Halloween. If they knew the whole story, they'd understand. I'm sure they would. If I can't go to the Halloween party with my friends, I'd rather not go at all.

I don't really care about my costume anymore, but Mom knows I borrowed it from Alex. She made me try it on yesterday. It was way too big.

"Take it with you to your grandmother's." Mom said. "Bet she could alter it to fit you."

I try on the costume for Grandma.

"Is everything okay, William?" Grandma asks as she sticks another pin into the side of the Gryffindor blazer.

I shrug.

"You seem a little glum lately." She smiles and slips off the blazer. "Maybe it's the gloomy weather."

I sit on the low stool beside the sewing machine Grandma keeps on a table in the corner of her study. She needs to take in the seams on the costume a lot. Alex and I are the same age, but he is so much bigger than me.

"I wish I was muscular like Alex," I say. "Maybe I should start lifting weights or something."

"Ah. So that's what's on your mind. You're perfect, William, and so is Alex. Your bodies just have different shapes. One isn't better than the other. I learned that the hard way when I was just a little older than you."

I perk up. "Another story Grandma? Is there something in the suitcase to go with it?"

"Yes. It's a pattern envelope. It has a picture of a girl in a skirt on the front."

I dig it out while Grandma clips loose threads and examines her work.

I hold up the pattern envelope. "Hate to say it, Grandma, but this skirt is super ugly."

She laughs. "I didn't get to pick the pattern. My home economics teacher did. We made the skirt in my high school sewing class."

18

Curvy

LAURA, 1968

"LAURA, YOU have such curvy hips," Miss Quick observed crisply. She whisked the measuring tape from around my buttocks and jotted her findings on a slip of paper. Then she announced my skirt size loudly enough for the whole class to hear. I wanted to sink into the floor.

Our home economics class was making skirts. Miss Quick measured us and recommended what size pattern to buy. By the time her orange and black measuring tape was back dangling around her wrinkled neck like some mathematical piece of jewellery, thirty-five girls in the class knew everyone else's clothing sizes.

I was just grateful mine hadn't been the biggest. Lavinia, a girl whose confidence I couldn't help but admire, had that honour. Lavinia curled her eyelashes, wore really short miniskirts, and already dated boys. She seemed proud of her size.

"OVER HERE, Laura." Annemarie and Dina, my two best friends, waved to me from their booth at Mike's Cafe.

I hurried to join them, trying to suck in my stomach as I sailed past some grade eleven boys smoking at a nearby table. Since we had moved into the brand-new house that Mom and Dad had custom built for us, I walked right by the Rocky Creek teen hangout on my way home from high school. It took lots of convincing for Mom to let me join my friends there once a week after school.

"What would you like today, Laura?" Mike Martin, the owner, came to take my order as soon as I slid into the booth with my friends.

"What are you having?" I asked Annemarie.

"Fries with gravy and a chocolate milkshake."

"I'm having a Mexican hat," Dina reported.

I thought about how much I'd like a Mexican hat, a donut whose hole had been filled with soft ice cream and drizzled in hot chocolate sauce. But I remembered my skirt size. "A 7up," I said to Mr. Martin.

"Are you sure?" He whisked up a full ashtray of cigarette butts and gave the table a swipe with a wet cloth while I thought a minute. Then he poised his pencil over his order pad.

"Just a 7up," I repeated. Both Annemarie and Dina were as thin as Twiggy and never worried about what they ate. It didn't seem fair.

We chatted about our English teacher, Mr. Graham. He wore paisley shirts and had a ponytail. "I love it when he plays Beatles songs in poetry class," Dina gushed as Mr. Martin set our orders down. "Mom says I can't buy their records because they cross the line of decency."

"Kind of like Olivia Hussey and Leonard Whiting did in *Romeo and Juliet*?" Annemarie asked.

Dina and I giggled.

The three of us had gone to Winnipeg on the Greyhound bus to see *Romeo and Juliet* at the Kings Theatre. Our parents weren't sure we should go, but we convinced them seeing *Romeo and Juliet* would be educational since were studying the Shakespeare play in Mr. Graham's class. Luckily, our parents didn't know both Romeo and Juliet were practically naked in some scenes.

"I read about Olivia Hussey in a movie magazine." Dina used her finger to swipe up a dollop of chocolate sauce. "Did you know she takes diet pills?"

"Why? She looks beautiful." I raised my eyebrows and sipped my 7up slowly.

"Franco Zeffirelli, the director of *Romeo and Juliet*, told her she was too curvy." Dina said.

"Would you take diet pills, Laura?" Annemarie speared another gravy-covered fry.

I fidgeted with the straw in my 7up. Had my friends noticed I wasn't as skinny as they were? "Do you think I need diet pills?"

Annemarie blushed. "No . . . no. It's just, with your father being a doctor, you could probably get a prescription easily."

I coughed and took a sip of my drink. "What are you guys doing this weekend? Want to go skating Saturday night?" I asked, changing the subject.

By the time Annemarie and Dina had cleaned their plates, we'd agreed to meet at the outdoor rink the next day at seven o'clock.

At supper, Marjorie talked about basketball tryouts. "I think I'm going to make the team, but I hope I don't have to decide between basketball and track."

Marjorie had inherited most of the athletic talent in our family. At the summer cottage we rented at Windward Lake, I'd become a pretty good swimmer. But Rocky Creek didn't have a swimming pool, so there weren't many chances to exercise my only sports skill.

Maybe if I was better at sports, I would be skinny like my sister.

Saturday morning, Marjorie and I woke up when we heard our parents' voices in the bathroom beside our bedroom. It was weigh-in time for Mom.

"Do you think she lost weight this week?" Marjorie whispered nervously.

"I hope so." I was worried for Mom and my hands shook as I straightened my quilt.

Our parents thought we were still sleeping. But we woke up early most Saturdays when we heard Mom arguing softly with Dad about getting on the scale. He weighed her once a week and recorded her diet progress in the little blue book Mom hid behind the rolls of toilet paper under the sink.

I was worried I needed to lose weight. But although I talked to Mom about everything, somehow this Saturday morning ritual with Dad made me uncomfortable bringing up the subject of my weight with her.

The scale squeaked and Dad said, "Oh dear, Virginia. You are up a bit. I really wish you would start taking those diet pills. I left a bottle here in the linen closet for you, just under the pillowcases. I wouldn't want the kids to find them."

"William, I am scared of those pills! Don't you like the way I look?"

"You are beautiful, Virginia, but being overweight can be dangerous. So many of my patients have health problems because of their weight. It worries me. You know heart attacks run in your family. What would the children and I do without you?"

"I'll think about it, William."

Mom and I went down to Rocky Creek Dry Goods on Saturday morning to pick up a pattern and material for my skirt. We settled on some black wool fabric with red vertical lines. Mom assured me the design would be slimming.

Mrs. Dorset, who ran the store, looked me up and down over the glasses pinching her nose before she cut my swatch of fabric. "Seems like you've filled out some lately, Laura. I'll add just a little extra material."

I studied an ant crawling along the floor. Did Mrs. Dorset think I was gaining weight too?

"I don't believe we'll need any extra material, Mrs. Dorset. But thank you." Mom spoke firmly as she removed a two-dollar bill from her wallet to pay.

I GOT to the skating rink that evening just a little before Dina and Annemarie arrived. Some grade twelve kids were there. Most of them were skating in guy-and-girl combos holding hands. I sat down on a bench to put on my skates.

"Hi, Laura." Gladys' skate blade raised a spray of ice as she stopped in front of me. She was the editor of the Rocky Creek Collegiate newspaper called *The Eye*. I'd been thrilled to get the job as a grade nine reporter in September.

"Hi, Gladys." My voice squeaked as I realized Don Davidson, the dreamiest boy in the senior class, was skating with Gladys.

"This is Laura," Gladys introduced me. "She's submitted some really great stories for the paper this year."

"You wrote the review of Zeffirelli's *Romeo and Juliet*, didn't you?" Don looked me in the eyes and smiled. "I liked the way you highlighted some of the minor characters."

"She also wrote a funny piece about her family's trip to Expo 67," Gladys added.

"I missed that one." Don smiled at me again. "I'll have to check it out."

Don and Gladys skated away. My heart was pounding. *Don Davidson talked to me! He liked my writing. Did he notice how bulky I looked in my parka, or was he fascinated with my grey-green eyes? Mom says they're my best feature.*

By the time Annemarie and Dina arrived, I was dying to share my news.

"That dreamboat Don Davidson just talked to me."

"How did he even know who you were?" Annemarie stopped lacing up her skates in surprise.

"Gladys introduced me. He said he'd read my *Romeo and Juliet* review in *The Eye*."

Dina sighed. "Don always reminds me of Neil Diamond."

The three of us skated around the rink holding hands. We were hoping one of the boys in grades ten or eleven would ask us to skate. We didn't want to look desperate though, so we laughed and talked together as if the boys didn't even matter.

And then we were coming up behind Gladys and Don.

"She's smart, but chubby."

I cringed. Don's voice. He was talking about me.

Dina and Annemarie exchanged glances and immediately started singing "Sealed with a Kiss" along with Gary Lewis and the Playboys, which was being belted out over the sound system.

My heart twisted. I knew my friends were trying to drown out Don. We skated by him, but he must not have noticed us because he kept talking.

"Her eyes are nice. She just needs to lose weight."

THAT NIGHT, Dad had to go to the hospital to perform an emergency surgery. After I heard him leave I had trouble sleeping. I kept thinking about what Don had said. Finally, I went into the bathroom, turned on the light, and looked at myself in the mirror. My "curvy" hips looked bigger than ever.

I opened the linen closet and stood on my tiptoes to take out the bottle of diet pills from behind the towels. I squinted to read the label. It said to take one at a time, but I figured I'd take a few extra just to get off to a good start. Hopefully Mom and Dad wouldn't check the bottle. Maybe by the time they found out some pills were gone, I would be looking so slim they'd think it was a good idea for me to take them.

I popped four of the pills into my mouth and cupped my hands under the tap to collect water to wash them down.

"LAURA! LAURA! Wake up!"

I opened my eyes. Marjorie was shaking me. She looked like she was on a fuzzy television screen. Her face was wobbling in front of mine.

"Laura, you were shouting so loudly you woke me up. I thought you were having a bad dream."

"Something's wrong," I mumbled. "My heart is pounding so fast."

"I'm getting Mom." Marjorie announced.

A few minutes later, I felt the bed sink as Mom sat down beside me. She felt my head and held my wrist to check my pulse.

"What's going on Laura? Did you skip supper? Did you overdo it at the skating rink? Tell me what's wrong." She looked so worried.

"Diet pills," I mumbled, "The ones Dad got for you. Maybe I swallowed too many."

"*Gott in Himmel*!" Mom cried, sounding just like Uncle Herman. "How many did you take?"

"Four."

"Oh, Laura! What possessed you to do such a thing? Don't you know how dangerous it is to take strange pills without a doctor's perscription?"

"But Dad's a doctor and he perscribed them for you!" I protested. Then I started to cry softly. "I'm so big, Mom. I needed one of the largest dress patterns in home economics class. I'm no good in sports, and at the skating rink tonight, I overheard Don Davidson say I was chubby."

"Laura, that's nonsense."

"I've always wanted to swim like you can." Marjorie says.

Mom took my hand. "You get such high grades at school. You're an excellent writer. Lots of girls would give anything for your lovely brown hair. You're not too big. You are just right. People's bodies change, you know. How your body looks at fourteen isn't how it is going to look when you are my age."

"But Dad thinks you're overweight, Mom!" As soon as I spoke, I wished I could grab the words back. But they'd escaped like runaway arrows and hit my sweet Mom. Her face fell. She got up and walked out of the room.

"I shouldn't have said that." My voice is pinched.

"You probably shouldn't have." Marjorie laid down in her bed.

During the week Mom didn't talk about what happened Saturday night. It was almost like it had been a nightmare. I looked for the diet pills on Monday, but they were gone from their spot in the linen closet.

The next Saturday, Marjorie and I woke up when Mom and Dad went into the bathroom for Mom's weekly weigh in.

"Time to step on the scale, Virginia," Dad said.

"No, William. I'm not getting on the scale today, and you are never going to ask me to do it again."

Marjorie and I looked at each other, our eyes wide.

"What's wrong?" Dad sounded as surprised as we were.

"I love you, William, and you know I'd do almost anything for you, but from now on my weight isn't going to be any of your business. I burned the little blue record book, and I flushed the diet pills down the toilet. And that's the last I want to hear about it. Don't ask me how much I weigh ever again."

We heard Mom's steps firm and sure on the linoleum as she marched out of the bathroom and closed the door not with a slam but a determined thud.

"Wow!" The word came out of my mouth and Marjorie's at almost the same time.

"Was that our mom?" Marjorie asked.

"I think it was." I sat up and slipped on my housecoat. "Let's go and see if we can convince Mom to make waffles with Grandma Annie's white sauce for breakfast."

"Great idea." Marjorie wriggled into her housecoat, and we headed downstairs.

19

Emergency

WILL

WALKING TO Grandma's on Wednesday number ten, I hum my piece for concert band tryouts. I've prepared as best I can. My chest tightens. I really hope both Aneesh and I get into the band, even though it might feel awkward sitting in the brass section with him when he won't talk to me. Every day, I look for a chance to try and explain things to him and Emmaline, but they are always busy with a bunch of other kids.

I let myself into Grandma's with my key. "I'm here, Grandma. What's for snack today?"

She doesn't answer, but as I set my school bag down, I hear a loud crash. Then a thud. My heart almost stops beating. I charge toward the sound and find Grandma lying in a crumpled heap on her walk-in closet floor. An overturned kitchen chair is beside her.

"Grandma!"

She doesn't answer. What if she's dead? I kneel beside her and she starts to moan but her eyes stay closed. There's blood on the floor. I take her hand. "Grandma, are you okay?"

She still doesn't answer.

I need to get help. I look around frantically for her phone. Then I notice it poking out from her sweatpants' pocket. I call Mom first, but it goes to messages right away. Right. It's Wednesday. She has a late lecture. She's silenced her phone. Next, I try Dad. He doesn't answer either. He must be in court.

I dial 911. I push my glasses up my nose and straighten my shoulders while I wait for someone to answer.

"Hello. This is 911. What is your emergency?"

"My grandmother is lying on the floor. She's bleeding, and she won't talk to me." I can hardly believe how cool and calm I sound as I give the operator my name and Grandma's address, just like I learned in that babysitting course.

The operator tells me an ambulance will come as quickly as it can.

Mendelssohn barks in the hallway. I run to the apartment door, yanking it open. Leon is standing there clipping on Mendelssohn's leash.

"Leon! Grandma's been hurt. I called the ambulance."

Worry washes over Leon's face. He and Mendelssohn hurry into the apartment with me. He kneels next to Grandma and shakes her arm gently. "Laura ... Laura."

Grandma moans and opens her eyes for a moment and then closes them again.

"Help is on the way, Laura." Leon takes Grandma's pulse and looks up at me. "It's a little fast, Will, but I think it's okay."

I cover Grandma's hand with mine. Leon stands up. "Will, why don't you and Mendelssohn stay with your grandmother? I'll go down to the lobby and wait for the ambulance.

I'll direct them up here when they arrive. I think it is best if she doesn't move at all, just in case something is broken."

A few minutes after Leon leaves, Grandma's eyes open. She tries to sit up, but I gently touch her shoulder. "Grandma, you shouldn't move until the ambulance gets here."

"So silly," Grandma mumbles. "Trying to get . . . jigsaw puzzle . . . top shelf. Chair slipped." She closes her eyes again and Mendelssohn lies down beside her, sticking his nose into the crook of her arm.

It seems to take forever for the ambulance to come. After they arrive, the paramedics put Grandma on a stretcher and wheel her outside. Leon and I follow the ambulance to the hospital in his car. It's hard to catch my breath as we drive. Fear is jamming up my lungs.

What if Grandma dies like Grandpa did?

I shake my head to erase the thought.

I pull Grandma's phone from my jacket pocket and call Mom and Dad again. This time, I get through. Leon stays with me till my parents arrive at the emergency department. Mom gives me a quick hug before taking Grandma's hand. The doctor comes over just then to share the test results with us.

"Nothing is broken," the doctor says. "We took some X-rays and ran a few tests." She turns to Grandma. "We had to put five stitches in your head, Laura, but they should heal nicely. I'd suggest you not be alone tonight since we need to watch for signs of a possible concussion."

"I'll spend the night at her place," Mom says.

"Can I hang out there too?" I ask.

Grandma and Mom both smile.

After we get Grandma safely home, Dad goes to pick up supper. While Mom answers work emails on her laptop at the dining room table, I sit beside Grandma, who is tucked in bed under the Circle of Time quilt.

"Dad's getting some sushi. I told him to order the rainforest roll you like so much, Grandma."

"I don't know if I'll be able to eat anything."

"He's getting miso soup too. You can try that. It will give you strength."

Grandma pats my arm. "I feel so foolish, William. I should have been more careful."

"I'm just glad you're okay. Full reveal, Grandma: I was terrified when I looked into the closet and found you lying there with all that blood on the floor."

"I understand how you must have felt, William. When I was just a few years older than you, my mom got really sick. My brothers and sister and I were terrified too."

"Grandma you don't have to tell me a story now. Wait till you feel better."

"I'd like to. It will make the time pass quickly until that medication the doctor prescribed kicks in and I can sleep. I promise I'll stop if I get too tired."

20

Should I Be Driving?

SOMETHING WAS wrong at our house. We kids didn't know what it was exactly, but things with Mom and Dad seemed different. Dad hadn't made a comment about the grocery bill being too high for weeks. Mom had stopped getting upset with Dad when he took phone calls from his patients during supper.

Marjorie and I talked about whether our family could be having money troubles. Frank thought our parents were sad because their good friends were getting divorced. Sweet Pete was sure Mom was sick.

But something was very wrong because usually on Sunday afternoons, Mom sat down at the piano and went into another world the minute her hands touched the keys. She filled the house with the notes of classy sonatas and the beat of jazzy forties tunes for hours. Now, after the Sunday lunch dishes were washed, Mom tinkered away at a listless song or two before wandering off to her bedroom for a nap.

A wan smile had replaced Mom's usual cheery chatter while she dished up our Red River cereal at breakfast. When she delivered the laundry to our rooms in the evening, she just placed our folded clothes on our beds without asking twenty questions about school and poking her nose into our homework.

She still drove us to the after-school activities jamming up our family calendar, but she winced when she was getting in and out of the car. She gripped the steering wheel like it was a life preserver. Frank and Marjorie and I didn't dare ask what was wrong. Maybe we didn't really want to know. Sweet Pete was only six and much braver.

As we sat eating our meat loaf and mashed potatoes for supper one night, he blurted out, "Mom, are you going to die?"

Mom looked at Dad and then he looked at us kids. "Mom has cancer," he said in his no-nonsense doctor voice. "She is seeing a specialist in Winnipeg. He recommended she have radiation treatments three times a week. The radiation will kill the cancer."

My fork clattered to my plate and sent bits of meat loaf skittering across the table. "Why didn't you tell us?"

Mom forced a smile. "We didn't want you to worry."

"So, you're not going to die?" Sweet Pete sounded like the TV lawyer, Perry Mason, demanding an answer from a witness.

"Of course, I'm not going to die." Mom grabbed a dish rag and cleaned up my meat loaf mess.

Frank studied the food on his plate as if it were a work of art.

"How long will you have the treatments, Mom?" Marjorie asked.

"For now, they've said three months. We'll have to see." Dad cut himself a thin slice of Mom's lemon meringue pie for dessert.

Frank pushed away from the table. "Excuse me. I have to get ready for my orchestra performance tonight."

"I forgot about that." Mom stood up. "Marjorie and Laura, can you help me clear the table? You girls can wash dishes. I'll drive Frank to the auditorium."

"I'll walk, Mom." Frank headed upstairs to get his violin.

"No. I'll take you, Frank," Mom called after him. "I want to hear you play. Just because I have cancer doesn't mean I am going to stop being your mother."

After Mom and Frank left, I filled the sink with water and put in lots of soap. As I washed, Marjorie dried the dishes. Mom had been asking Dad for a dishwasher for over a year now, but he'd always said they were too expensive. To our surprise just last week, he'd ordered a brand-new Maytag from Rocky Creek Furniture and Appliances. It was due to arrive soon.

"I bet Dad was feeling bad about Mom's cancer," Marjorie says, drying a glass. "That's why he finally bought the dishwasher. He must be worried to spend all that money. Just think, we won't have to wash dishes anymore."

"I'd rather Mom wasn't sick than have a dishwasher," I snapped.

Marjorie glared at me. Tears welled in her eyes and raced down her cheeks, dripping onto the tea towel in her hand. That got me going, and soon my tears were popping the soap bubbles in the sink. Marjorie and I didn't say anything. We just kept doing the dishes, our tears leaking all over everything.

If people had watched our family over the next few weeks, we would have seemed the same as always. Dad said not to tell people about Mom's cancer just yet, and at first, we didn't. After we left for school every Monday, Wednesday, and Friday, Mom made the hour-long drive into Winnipeg for her treatments.

As I sat in history class and worked on my project about John F. Kennedy, I tried to imagine what the machine zapping Mom's cancer looked like. When I opened *Brave New World* in English class, I wondered if Mom was scared when she went into the radiation room. While eating the ground beef and mayonnaise sandwich Mom had made for my lunch, I wondered if cancer was something you inherited. Could I get it too? As I sang "You'll Never Walk Alone" in the choir and reached the line about holding your head high in a storm, my voice crackled on the descant. Would Mom survive her cancer storm?

After Mom's fourth week of treatments, Marjorie and I were more worried than ever. We talked in whispers in our bedroom.

"Mom looks so tired."

I nod. "I think she left the supper table to throw up. I followed her upstairs and listened at the bathroom door."

Marjorie kicked her slippers off and slid under her quilt. "She forgot to read Sweet Pete his Hardy Boys chapter tonight. I heard him crying, so I went and read to him and listened to his prayers. He prayed for Mom to get better."

I went to the window and stared at the autumn leaves piling up on the yard. "I know this is selfish, but I'm wondering who will help me practise for my driver's licence next year when I turn sixteen if Mom can't." I lowered my voice. "Mom and Dad don't know this, but Uncle Herman has been letting me drive his truck in the field for a few summers now. That's been good practice, but driving on the streets of Rocky Creek will be a lot different."

Marjorie sighed. "Mom is too tired to come to my curling games. It just isn't the same without her there to clap and yell 'sweep.'"

"You used to hate it when she yelled 'sweep,'" I reminded Marjorie.

"I know. Now I miss it."

"Maybe we need to learn to cook, Marjorie. We've been having TV dinners a lot. They taste like cardboard." I got into bed. "Dad seems to be working harder than ever. He's off to do surgery in the morning before we get up, and he's always missing supper because his office hours run late."

Marjorie turned off the lamp on the nightstand between our twin beds. "I think it's hard for him to be around Mom right now. He's a doctor, but he can't handle it when someone he loves is sick. Remember how Mom had to call Doctor Calder when you had appendicitis because Dad was so emotional?"

I whispered in the dark. "Do you think Frank is okay? He's always watching Mom like she's an actress in *The Twilight Zone* and he can't take his eyes off her till he finds out how the episode ends."

Some nights Marjorie and I talked so late about Mom that we heard the clock chime midnight.

Eventually, Mom's three closest friends—Arlene, Iris, and Lily—found out about the cancer. They must have told other people. When Mom was about a month and a half into her treatments, casseroles and cakes and coleslaws appeared on the kitchen counter every day. The ladies from the church slipped in each afternoon while Mom rested and left supper for us. The food wasn't the same as Mom's, but it was a whole lot better than TV dinners.

And then one morning, just as we were about to leave for school, Iris walked into our house. "I'm driving you to Winnipeg for your treatment today, Virginia." She took Mom's arm, walked her outside, and eased Mom into her big Buick.

Frank, Marjorie, Sweet Pete, and I waved good-bye as the car sailed down the street.

After that, mom's friends took turns driving her to Winnipeg. Our days, and weeks, and eventually two months, slipped into a numb kind of existence. It felt like we were sleepwalking through a silent movie.

One morning, I had just reached the end of the driveway on my way to school when Mom called my name. I turned to see her standing in the front doorway.

"Laura, come back please."

I ran across the lawn to her.

"Iris just called. Her mother had a bad fall, and she needs to take her in to emergency. She can't drive me to Winnipeg today. It's too late to ask anyone else or I'll be late for my appointment. But I don't think I can go alone. You'll have to come with me."

"Sure, Mom." I was a little sad. Miss Mulvey had asked me to read my latest story aloud in English class, and in choir, we had started rehearsals for this year's musical, *The Pirates of Penzance*.

Mom backed the car out of the garage, and I slipped into the passenger seat beside her. By the time we were driving down the highway, Mom was almost her usual self, doling out twenty questions.

"How are musical rehearsals coming along?"

"Is math class getting any easier?"

"How are things going with Annemarie and Dina?"

Mom told me a funny story about a naughty pig on their farm growing up and I sang a number from *The Pirates of*

Penzance for her. Mom knew it too and chimed in with her alto voice.

After she parked the car at the St. Boniface Hospital, Mom gave me a dollar bill. "Why don't you go to the cafeteria and wait for me there, Laura. You can order some lunch."

"Are you sure you don't want me to come with you, Mom?"

"No. They won't allow you in anyway."

I hugged Mom and watched her go into the elevator.

I didn't think I'd be able to eat anything right away because my stomach was fidgety with worry. I wandered around the familiar area. I found our old building easily—the one we had lived in when Dad was studying to be a doctor. I even spotted our apartment window. I thought about what our lives were like then, before Sweet Pete was even born, when Frank was the baby of the family. I was in grade one and rode the city bus to school.

After I ordered an egg salad sandwich and a Mountain Dew in the cafeteria, I read another chapter of *Brave New World*, which was tucked in my school bag. Then I made notes on the next chapter in my history textbook. I was just finished when Mom walked through the cafeteria door. She moved slowly and carefully, as if she had to think about every step.

"Are you okay, Mom?" I hurried over to her. Her face was whiter than Annemarie's and mine had been after we'd slathered ourselves with cold cream during a sleepover.

"Yes. I'll be fine." Mom's voice quavered. She took my hand as we exited the hospital and slowly walked across the parking lot to our latest Mercury Marquis. Mom's steps weren't steady. She might have fallen if she hadn't been gripping my fingers.

I helped her slide in behind the steering wheel. "Mom, are you sure you are going to be all right?"

Her hands shook as she searched for the car keys in her big black purse. "Just give me a minute." She took a couple of deep breaths and slipped the *Ford Family of Fine Music* eight-track tape into the player. Then she shifted the car into drive and pulled onto Tache Avenue. We didn't even try and talk over Henry Mancini singing "Born Free" and Floyd Cramer playing "Up, Up and Away" on the tape. By the time we reached the highway, Mom's face had turned green.

Suddenly, she jerked the car onto the shoulder and turned down a country road. She pulled to the side. Gravel sprayed up behind us and pinged on the car trunk as she brought the Mercury to an abrupt halt. She wrenched open her door and threw up all over the road.

My heart pounded faster than when I'd taken those diet pills. What should I do? I figured Mom and I needed help. With clammy hands, I scrounged around in my school bag for the napkins I'd stuffed into it at the cafeteria.

"Here you go, Mom." I tried to hand Mom a napkin, but she looked so helpless I wiped the vomit off her face myself.

"I think you will have to drive, Laura," Mom whispered.

"I can't drive, Mom," I said, my voice filled with fear.

Mom winced.

"I'm not even old enough for my learner's licence. Isn't it illegal for me to drive?"

"We will stick to the country roads so people don't see us. I will tell you exactly what to do and where to go."

I pointed to a couple of farms nearby. "Maybe I should go to one of those houses and ask to use the phone to call Dad."

"He's busy, Laura. You can do this. You are a brave, smart girl and you've driven Uncle Herman's truck in the field when he's combining."

"You knew about that?"

"Grandma Annie told me last year. I wasn't very happy with your uncle right then, but now I'm glad he taught you how to drive."

"Uncle Herman's truck was a stick shift, Mom."

"Driving an automatic transmission is easier, Laura."

"What if we have an accident?"

"If I keep driving, we will have one for sure."

Mom got out of the car and walked around to the passenger side holding onto the hood and the side of the Mercury like it was a crutch. She opened my door.

"Slide over, Laura."

I obeyed, but my heart was pounding so hard I was sure Mom must hear it. I clutched the steering wheel with a vice-like grip stop my hands from shaking.

"Do you know how to put it into drive?" Mom rested her hand on the gear shift.

"I think so." I took a deep breath and moved the shift to the letter *D*.

"Okay. Now press the gas pedal, easy at first, and pull onto the gravel. No one is coming."

I gave it a little too much gas, and the car lurched across the road and almost went into the ditch on the opposite side, but I soon got things under control. I was scared to drive too fast. The Mercury puttered along down the different country roads, following Mom's directions.

"We are definitely taking the scenic route," I said, trying to lighten the mood.

Mom smiled. "You're doing great, Laura."

Her words slurred. That scared me.

"I remember when my dad taught me how to drive," Mom said. "He made me learn how to change a tire too."

Even though she was obviously bone tired, Mom talked all the way back to Rocky Creek.

"Did I ever tell you about the time our caboose tipped in the snow and I got a black eye . . .?"

"I am so proud you are a reporter, Laura. I bet some day you will edit the school paper . . ."

"I don't want you kids to worry. I will get better . . ."

"I'll never forget the time the chandelier fell down on the table in the farmhouse right between Grandma and me . . ."

"Laura, you are getting so tall. I love how you look in that new dress we ordered from the Sears catalogue . . ."

"I know it's hard for Sweet Pete not to have me doing as many things for him. I'm proud of the way you and Marjorie and Frank are stepping in to help out."

Dozens of times, Mom repeated how everything would be fine, how she would get better, how our family was going to be okay—like a needle stuck in the groove of a record on a turntable.

Luckily, we didn't pass any other cars. A few times, the Mercury got away on me, but I always managed to keep control. When we finally pulled onto our driveway, Mom looked like she could barely keep her eyes open. I helped her up to her bedroom and tucked her under the covers.

Just before I closed the door she said, "I love you, Laura. You were so brave today. Just remember, you can never tell Dad about this."

And I never did. Not even when Mom got so much sicker that they had to stop the treatments. Not even when we were all called to the hospital one night to say good-bye to her. Not even when she miraculously got better and finally came back home.

Right after I turned sixteen, I took my driver's test. I'd only had my beginner's licence for two weeks.

"You learned to drive pretty fast," the tester remarked as he looked at my application. "Who taught you?"

"My mother," I told him. "She has lots of confidence in me."

21

The Whole Story

WILL

WE HAVE concert band tryouts on Wednesday morning.
The conductor says she'll post the list of kids who got in at
noon. I head for the bulletin board outside the music room
right after lunch feeling shaky and nervous. What happens
if I don't make the cut?

That unsettled feeling gets worse when I see Emmaline and Aneesh looking at the list. They've been giving me
the silent treatment again for a couple of weeks now. The
thought of approaching them makes my stomach knot. I
turn to walk away, but then I think of Grandma. She didn't
walk away from snowstorms or a stranded deer or an injured
dog. I push my glasses up my nose, straighten my shoulders,
and march right up to the board.

The list is alphabetical by last name. I spot *Aneesh Prasad*
about halfway down. *Will Sanders* is right below it. All right!
Happiness surges through me.

"Way to go, Aneesh!" I say, clapping him on the back. When I realize what I've done, my stomach clenches, but Aneesh doesn't pull away.

Instead, he turns and looks at me. "Same to you, Will."

I can't believe it. Aneesh finally spoke to me!

Emmaline puts her hand on my arm. "I knew you would make it, Will."

"Thanks, Emmaline," I say.

After school, I am surprised to see Emmaline and Aneesh sitting on the basketball court bleachers where we always meet.

My steps slow as I get closer, but I keep walking.

They both look uncomfortable, shifting on the bleacher seats and scuffling their feet on the pavement.

"We miss you, Will," Emmaline says.

I stop walking, and my cheeks flush. "I miss you guys too."

"Maybe we should talk," Aneesh mumbles.

I drop onto the bleacher seat a few feet away from them. The bleacher reminds me of the bench in the locker room, the one where . . .

I put my head in my hands. I don't want to think about it. My chest grows tighter and tighter, as if there's a big rubber band around it. "I-I . . . I only told you part of what happened with those bullies Gregory and Grayson," I stutter.

They look at me like they're waiting for more.

"They . . ." I gulp. "They'd knock off my cap and steal my glasses and throw my lunch in the trash bin. They'd punch me in the chest or stomach, trip me during soccer practice . . . and they got the rest of the team to pick on me too." I turn my head away and blink back tears. "Once, after a practice..." I take a deep breath. "They stole my clothes when I was in the shower and... and they left Grandma's book *Why Are You Naked?* where my clothes had been."

Emmaline gasps. "Where were your coaches and teachers?"

I shake my head. "They never saw." Just remembering everything that happened makes me feel like I'm drowning, and I start to panic. But this time, I have to tell the whole story.

Emmaline scoots over and puts her arm around me. "Oh, Will."

Aneesh stares at the ground.

"After that..." Sweat drips from my forehead and I start gasping for air.

"Just take your time, Will," Emmaline says, her arm still around me.

Aneesh doesn't say anything, but his face is getting red.

"The punching and stuff got worse, and then they started asking me for money," I stumbled on. "They said if I didn't pay them they'd get their big brothers to put bad things on the internet about Grandma. They'd make fun of her books so people would stop buying them."

Aneesh looks up. "Why didn't you tell your parents?"

"How could I?" I sob, my lungs bursting. "How would Grandma feel if she found out her books got me into trouble? I just started giving Gregory and Grayson my allowance every week until we moved here."

"That's awful, Will." Emmaline says softly. "Truly awful."

"That's why I didn't want anyone here to find out about Grandma," I say, my voice catching. "Not even you. That's why I didn't say anything when you thought she was dead. I figured it would be easier, that I wouldn't have to think about any of it again or worry about bullies at this school finding out about her. I know I should have told you, but Grandma lived in Rocky Creek then, and I thought you'd never meet her anyway."

"I get that," Emmaline says. "I'm so sorry this happened to you."

Aneesh lifts his head and looks directly at me. "First of all, Will, if you ever have to deal with bullies at this school, you won't be alone. Emmaline and I have your back. No matter what."

"And secondly, Will," Emmaline chimes in, "you can trust us with any secret."

"I know that now. But I was so scared. Everything all tumbled together, and once I started making up lies about Wednesdays, I didn't know how to tell you the truth."

Aneesh moves over, so I'm sandwiched between him and Emmaline. The tightness around my chest loosens, and this huge knot of worry that's been twisting up inside me since the beginning of September starts to untangle.

We sit there, all quiet, for a minute. Then I look at my watch.

"I've got to go to Grandma's now," I say.

"Can we come along?" Emmaline asks. "She did say we could visit anytime."

"I'd like you to, but Grandma had an accident last week. She fell off a chair and needed some stitches."

"Oh no, Will. Is she okay?" Emmaline looks worried.

"She's fine, but I should maybe ask her if she's ready for company before you visit."

"Sounds good." Aneesh says.

They wave good-bye and I head off to Grandma's with a hopeful bounce in my step.

GRANDMA IS meditating in the living room when I get there. She points her chin at the video on the television. "Just three more minutes left."

I go into the washroom and splash cold water in my eyes so Grandma won't suspect I've been crying. Then I wander into the study and stare at the suitcase in the corner. I open it and find a pair of silver car keys. They jingle as I walk back into the living room.

Grandma is rolling up her mediation rug. She looks up and smiles. "I see you found the keys to our old Mercury Marquis. Pretty obvious they went with last week's story."

I smile. "How are you feeling Grandma?"

"Fine. My stitches are itchy, but they'll dissolve soon."

"Emmaline and Aneesh want to come along with me next week. Would that be okay with you?"

Grandma smiles. "More than okay." She goes into the kitchen and takes a pan of brownies out of the oven and sets them on the stovetop to cool.

"Grandma, I'm curious about the stuff in your suitcase. They aren't just a bunch of random things, are they?"

"No, they're not. When I was cleaning out our house after Grandpa died, I found all kinds of memorabilia from my childhood that I'd forgotten I even had. I was in a such a sad place, missing Grandpa. Writing always makes me feel better, so I started selecting a few of the items and writing down the stories they brought to mind."

"Have you ever thought about making a book out of those stories?" I ask.

"Would kids want to read them?"

"Emmaline and Aneesh and I love your sixties girl stories, Grandma. They can hardly wait to come over and hear another one."

"But they wouldn't be for young children like my other books."

"No, they wouldn't, but your sixties stories are perfect for kids my age."

"I'll have to think about that, William."

"You should." I can't believe I just said that! For the past few years, I've tried to hide what Grandma does for a living and now I'm asking her to publish a book!

Grandma interrupts my thought. "Would you like to pick another item for a story?"

I go into the study and pull something that resembles a tree branch from the suitcase. It's about the length of my forearm and looks like a piece of an antler. Grandma hates hunting, so I'm really curious about this one. "Grandma, is this part of an antler?"

Grandma nods. "It's from a deer."

"Where did you get it?"

"As a matter a fact, William, I shot that deer."

"Wow!" It's like I'm seeing Grandma as a totally new person. I wouldn't have guessed in a million years that she did some of the stuff she's talked about in her stories.

"Listen, William, I need to ice these brownies and change. Come into the study and I'll let you read the story that goes with the deer antler." She smiles. "This is your eleventh story, isn't it? I've enjoyed every moment of our time together these past weeks."

"Me too."

Grandma sits down in front of the computer on her desk and opens a file named "Lullaby for Laura." She sighs. "I was at Uncle Herman's farm when this happened—just as my week-long summer visit was coming to an end. Only Uncle Herman, Grandma Annie, and I were at the farm that day. Lillian wasn't living at home anymore because she had a job in Saskatoon, and Aunt Eudora had left early in the morning to drive Fern to a summer camp several hundred miles away. She was going to come back the next day."

As Grandma leaves, I sit down in her desk chair and start reading.

22

Lullaby
for Laura

LAURA, 1970

UNCLE HERMAN and I were driving back out to the farm
from town. We'd picked up some flour for Grandma Annie's
strawberry pies at the general store and a part for Uncle Herman's combine from the John Deere dealer.

Neither of us saw the young buck until it shot across
the highway.

"*Gott in Himmel!*" Uncle Herman shouted. He slammed
on the brakes and turned the steering wheel just as the car
and the creature collided. The Studebaker careened off the
road and came to a dead stop in the ditch.

Stunned, I sucked in a long breath. One of the deer's
antlers had gone right through the windshield and pushed
against my cheek. I wondered for just a moment how the
antler could feel fuzzy like a peach's skin, but at the same
time, as hard as its pit.

"Are you hurt, Laura?" my uncle's voice wavered. He used his left hand to pry the bleeding fingers of his right off the steering wheel. His eyes welled with worry as he looked at me. "Is anything broken?"

I edged my head very carefully away from the antlers and leaned back. My heart was thumping and my head throbbed.

"Can you move your legs?"

I wiggled my toes in my scuffed white sandals with silver buckles. My voice wobbled. "I'm fine, Uncle Herman. Are you okay?"

"What's that?" Uncle Herman pointed to a growing stain on my bell-bottom pants.

I rolled them up and gasped when I saw a gash as jagged as a saw blade on my knee. It wasn't a very deep wound but I gagged at the sight of so much blood and hoped I wouldn't vomit.

Uncle Herman shifted awkwardly and pulled a giant white handkerchief out of his pants pocket. "Here. Tie this around that cut."

I took the handkerchief and wrapped it around my knee. The fancy blue *H* Fern had embroidered into the handkerchief's corner swam in front of my eyes. I didn't realize I was crying till a few tears splashed onto my hand.

Uncle Herman tried to open his car door. The handle didn't seem to be working. He leaned his left shoulder into the window. With a grunt and a mighty push, the door crashed to the ground. Uncle Herman nearly fell out with it.

He carefully swung his legs to the ground beside the car and then came around to my side. He opened the door for me.

We both sat down in the ditch where the car had landed. Pictures of what had just happened flashed through my brain like a film projector gone mad. I shook my head to clear away the frightening images.

We sat for a minute in the evening heat, catching our breath as our heartbeats slowed after their fearful spike. The bristly stubble lining the ditch poked my behind.

"Someone will come along soon," my uncle reassured me. "They will give us a ride or go and phone for help."

I nodded, not trusting my voice to say anything.

The evening was filled with summer sounds, but they seemed strangely soft after the loud crash. Mosquitoes whined and bullfrogs croaked. The slightest breeze rustled the leaves on stands of birch bordering both sides of the highway.

I heard an agonized gasp. It was the deer, his antler still lodged in the windshield. His chest heaved as he gulped for air. Mangled front legs and a huge gaping hole in his side leaked blood all over the car hood. It dripped down the front fender and pooled in the ditch.

I turned my head away. I couldn't stand to look at all that pain.

Uncle Herman staggered to his feet and limped over to the car. "This deer's in a bad way, Laura. We have to help him. Can't let him suffer like this."

Bracing himself on the Studebaker, Uncle Herman made his way around the back of it and up to the steering wheel. He pulled the keys out of the ignition and hobbled to the trunk. He fit the key into its lock. A cloud of flour rose from the trunk as it opened, covering Uncle Herman in a white mist.

"I guess Grandma's pies are going to have to wait," Uncle Herman said licking the flour off his lips. "The Robin Hood bag split wide open."

I watched my ghostly pale uncle take his rifle out of the trunk. He tried to unlock the safety with his right hand, but his bloody fingers wouldn't cooperate. I winced just watching him.

"You are going to have to help me, Laura. I can't hold my rifle steady with this damaged hand of mine."

"What do you want me to do?" I asked in a blur of panic.

"We've got to shoot this poor creature. He's in so much pain. It's not right."

"Oh, Uncle Herman. I don't think I can do that."

"Laura, you've been target shooting in the pasture with me for years. You hit those cans every time."

I protested, my voice rising a note with every word. "But tin cans are just metal. This deer is a living thing."

"Yes, and that's why we have to help him. We *have to*, Laura."

I walked stiffly towards Uncle Herman, the gash in my knee sending a spiderweb of prickly pain down my leg. Uncle Herman held the rifle in his left hand and put his right hand around my shoulder, as much to support himself as to steady me. I could feel his bloody fingers leaving a wet imprint on the sleeve of my grey sweater.

We lurched towards the deer together. When we reached the front of the car, Uncle Herman lifted the rifle and helped me cradle it against my shoulder. I looked at the deer's head through the scope. Its eyes were wild and dark, like the deer we'd seen struggling in Windward Lake that summer long ago. I could feel its fear. It was a living thing.

"You need to aim for the heart, Laura. It is just above the front leg there."

I focused the rifle's sight on the spot but I couldn't shoot. Tears trickled down my face. "Uncle Herman, do we have to kill him? Isn't there any other way to help him?'

"I'm afraid not, my child. He's hurt too badly."

"What if we just leave him to die? He would die, wouldn't he?" My voice sounded panicky, and my breath came out in short puffs.

"Yes, I'm afraid he would, but his death would be slow and painful and full of suffering. We can at least make it easier for him."

"You're sure we need to do this?"

"Yes, Laura. Now take a deep breath, just like I taught you. Relax, child."

I inhale slowly and calm my heart.

"Now, let out half the breath, squeeze the trigger, and follow through." Uncle Herman's hand was sure and steady on my shoulder. I let out my ragged breath and fired.

The bullet landed with a thud. A shudder rippled through the buck's body. Then he lay still. Oh, so still.

I turned my head away.

"Good girl," Uncle Herman gently took the rifle from me. "Good girl."

We were so focused on the deer that we didn't even notice the grain truck till it was just a few metres away. It slowed as it reached us and stopped. My aunt and uncle's neighbour, Mr. Carver, jumped down from the cab.

"Herman, what happened?" Mr. Carver strode over to where we were still standing by the car's front bumper, frozen in place. His eyes grew wide when he saw the rifle and the dead young buck on the hood.

"You okay?" he asked my uncle.

Uncle Herman nodded slowly.

Mr. Carver turned to me, his eyes warm and troubled. "And you, Laura?"

Somehow, his kind face full of worried wrinkles cracked my heart and I started to sob in big hiccups that shuddered through my body in waves. I couldn't stop.

Later that night, when I was ready for bed, Grandma Annie came into my room to tell me she had called my parents. They would come tomorrow to take me home.

Even though Grandma hadn't tucked me into bed for a couple years now, I think she knew I needed it tonight. She smoothed the Circle of Time quilt and covered my hand with hers as I burrowed deeper into the snowy sheets smelling fresh from the clothesline.

"Do you think that deer had a soul, Grandma?

"I think it did, Laura. Don't worry. You did the right thing. You ended his pain. That was very brave. The kindest thing you could have done."

"Grandma, I know I'm too old for this, but I think I need a lullaby tonight."

"No one is ever too old for a lullaby." Grandma stroked my hair and began to sing "Schlaf, Kindlein, Schlaf."

23

The Right Thing

WILL

GRANDMA IS SO excited that I brought Emmaline and Aneesh along today. She's wearing the dangly earrings she bought on her trip to Bali, a flouncy skirt, and her red silk blouse. She never dresses up like that for me! She's gone all out for our snack too, baking three kinds of muffins, serving them on a silver tray, and setting the table with the china plates she inherited from her mother.

"Will told us about your shooting-the-deer story," Aneesh says, as he slathers marmalade on his muffin.

"I can't stop thinking about it," Emmaline adds.

"I still think about it a lot too, even though it happened so many years ago," Grandma says.

"Was it even legal for a kid like you to use a gun?" I ask.

Grandma traces the rim of her plate with her finger. "The rules weren't as strict in the 1960s as they are today. Most farmers had guns to kill gophers who ate their crops or wild animals who threatened their livestock."

"Did you like shooting?" Aneesh asks helping himself to yet another muffin.

"I admit I was always fearful about it, but it was something my Uncle Herman really wanted to teach me. I didn't have the heart to tell him I'd rather not."

"He also showed you how to drive a truck when he really shouldn't have," I say.

"Yes, he did. But times were different then, William. Most rural kids drove equipment to help with their family's farm work."

"Did you ever use a rifle again after you shot that deer?" Aneesh asks.

Grandma refolds the napkin beside her plate. "No, I never did. Having to kill that deer is one of the saddest and hardest things I've ever had to do in my life."

"Do you still think it was the right thing to do?" I wonder softly.

"Yes, I do."

Sharing my bullying story with Emmaline and Aneesh was one of the hardest things I ever had to do. But I knew it was the right thing for our friendship. "Grandma, how do you know if the things you decide to do are right?"

Grandma twists the wedding ring on her finger. "There is no sure way to know. You just do the best you can. I certainly haven't always done the right thing."

"Really?" Emmaline sounds surprised.

"A good example would be the night of my graduation dance."

"I want to hear that one," Aneesh says.

"I bet this story goes with the graduation hat in the suitcase," I say.

"Yes, it does."

"Did you have a date for this dance?" Emmaline wonders. "My big sister is going to her graduation dance this spring, and she's already worried about not having a date."

"I certainly did have a date. My high school boyfriend's name was Levi."

"You had a boyfriend before Grandpa?" I ask. "What happened to this Levi guy?"

"Levi went to study in Halifax the year after we graduated, and we just lost touch. It was hard to keep up a long-distance relationship in those days, William. We didn't have text messaging or email, and telephoning was very expensive."

Aneesh leans forward. "So, what happened at your graduation dance?"

"Let me tell you."

24

Paris Girl

LAURA, 1971

I PUSHED the heavy gold curtains apart just enough to see the kaleidoscope of colourfully dressed graduates and their proud parents crowding the Rocky Creek Collegiate gym. Black and gold balloons rose into the air from the centrepieces at each of the banquet tables around the room. As I waited backstage to make my speech, I stood for a moment, just listening. The din of happy, excited chatter echoed off the steel girders criss-crossing the ceiling.

My boyfriend, Levi, caught my eye. He gave me an enthusiastic thumbs up, his athletic shoulders straining the seams of his Sunday suit. Mom sat next to him. She spotted me too, and waved discreetly, patting her hair. She'd gone to the beauty shop that afternoon to have it styled in a new upsweep, just for tonight. Dad was chatting with the mayor of Rocky Creek, who was seated at the table next to ours.

Mr. Epstein, our history teacher and the master of ceremonies, adjusted his yellow bow tie and pushed his thick-black-framed glasses up his nose as he walked towards the podium. He tapped the mike several times and it popped over the sound system. "Ladies and gentlemen. Can I have your attention, please." He waited till everyone quieted down. "I am pleased this evening to introduce to you Laura Johnson, vice-president of the student council and editor of the Rocky Creek Collegiate newspaper, *The Eye*. She has been selected by her classmates to give the official senior farewell."

A twinge of disappointment struck me as I made my way across the stage. I had hoped to win the vote for valedictorian, but deep down, I knew that honour would, as usual, go to a boy. And it had—to Reggie Banks, the basketball team captain.

I was determined to make my farewell speech more personal than the one Reggie had given at the graduation ceremony earlier that afternoon. I pushed back my shoulders as Mom always reminded me to do. I was feeling pretty confident in my beautiful gown with its red velvet sash and embroidered skirt. Traditionally, the farewell speech was a long list of thank yous to the adults who had helped the graduates get through twelve years of education. Instead, I was going to pay tribute to my classmates.

As I reached the podium, the room fell silent, and I began. "Good evening, teachers, parents, and special guests ... but most of all, good evening to the fabulous kids in the class of 1971."

I looked out over the audience. Every single eye was on me. It was a powerful feeling to hold the attention of all those people. I took a deep breath and smoothly delivered my opening remarks, moving quickly to begin my list of thanks yous to my classmates.

"Thanks to all the athletes and sports teams who made games and competitions so exciting to watch...

"Thanks to all the singers and actors who put on such thrilling performances for us...

"Thanks to all the writers and photographers whose hard work resulted in the best school paper and yearbook ever."

I went on, gathering confidence as I called out the names individuals who had achieved greatness that year. A cheer went through the crowd when I mentioned the school's best athletes, artists, scientists, and journalists. I made sure to include kids from every group, many of whom had become my close friends over the past few years. I was feeling exhilerated, excited, and confident. I couldn't stop smiling—that is, until I looked out into the crowd and my eyes fell on a girl standing in the back corner of the room, by the exit.

Gloria Martinez.

She was looking at me with pure hatred—jaw tight, hands clenched into fists. Everything about her manner taunted me with anger and defiance. She kept her stormy eyes on me even as she briskly wiped a tear from her cheek with the back of her hand.

My smile froze on my face, and I nearly lost my place. Luckily, I'd rehearsed my speech a million times and managed to keep going, fixing my eyes on Levi and Mom, who were both beaming with pride. I finished my speech, but not with the flourish I'd hoped for.

As I made my way back to our table, people clapped and cheered and said "way to go" and "great speech." But even as I nodded and smiled, I couldn't get Gloria's fuming face out of my head. I craned my neck to the exit where she'd been standing, but she was gone.

"HEY, DID any of you happen to talk to Gloria tonight?" I turned to look at Annemarie, who sat in the backseat of Levi's car with her brother, George.

"Gloria who?" George asked, at the same time as Annemarie said, "Gloria Martinez?" She looked at me curiously. "No, I didn't see her. Was she even there?"

"She was there all right." I said. "I saw her at the back of the room while I was making my speech. She looked... I don't know how else to describe it. She looked like she hates my guts!"

"I find that very hard to believe!" Levi laughed. "Who could ever hate a sweet girl like you?" He ruffled my hair and popped in the Three Dog Night cassette tape and tapped his fingers to the beat of "Joy to the World." Then he turned his Dodge Dart out of the school parking lot. We were on our way to Winnipeg for a Rocky Creek graduation tradition, a midnight cruise down the Red River on the *Paddlewheel Princess*.

"No, I swear, you guys! Gloria was mad." I turned down the volume on Three Dog Night. "Mad at *me*! I have no idea what I could have done to offend her!"

"That's crazy, Laura," Annemarie reasoned. "Why would she be mad at you? You don't even talk to her!"

I turned around and stared at Annemarie. I was about to protest that of course I talked to Gloria! I was friendly with everyone in our grade. That's what my whole speech had been about! But then it hit me. My speech. I thought I'd been so inclusive, thanking people from every clique. But it never occurred to me that I might be leaving some people out.

George loosened his tie and ran his hands through his curly blond hair. "Was she in any of your classes, Laura?"

"We took chemistry together, " I said quietly, "and once or twice she was my partner for an experiment, but we never really chatted."

"I think she's going to be on the cruise," Annemarie reported. "A bunch of girls are coming in a group because they didn't get dates. I might have been one of them if it hadn't been for good old George here." Annemarie gave her brother a playful punch on the arm.

WE ARRIVED at the riverboat parking lot around 10:30. The moon lit up everything—the trees, the nearby Provencher Bridge, and the big, old houses on the other bank. It felt like we were on a movie set. Lots of kids were on board already, and I could hear and feel the loud, pumping beat of the music even before we got out of the car. The four of us put our arms around each other and sang along, full throated, with Carole King's "I Feel the Earth Move" as we danced our way to the boat.

We found an empty table in the middle of the noisy room filled with laughing kids. A few guys from the gymnastics teams were cartwheeling across the dance floor.

"Can I get you something to drink, Laura?" Levi took off his burgundy velvet tuxedo jacket and draped it across the back of his chair.

"I'll have a Coke."

Right when Levi was setting our drinks down, the boat gave a groaning lurch and pulled away from the dock. Coke splashed onto the white tablecloth. I'd only taken a few sips of my drink when the band broke into "Sweet Caroline." Levi shouted, "Let's celebrate!" and he pulled me up and away to the dance floor.

A couple of hours later, I had almost managed to forget about Gloria, but I was ready for some fresh air. Levi was in such great shape he could literally dance the night away. But I needed a break, so while he was doing the limbo with guys from his track team, I went out onto the deck.

The night air was refreshingly cool after all that dancing, and the river ran dark and smooth and deep around the boat. We were far from downtown Winnipeg now, and the only electric lights were those flickering on people's back porches. The moon lit up twisted tree roots along the bank. A flock of bats winged towards a branch to rest.

I thought I was alone on the deck, but as my eyes got used to the dark, I saw Gloria up near the bow to my left. I was suddenly struck by how beautiful she was, with her dark hair, regal expression, and long legs. She was always well-dressed, but didn't follow trends like the rest of us. She was easily the prettiest girl in our grade, and yet here she was on graduation night, all alone without a group of friends or even a date. Not that being pretty automatically made you popular, but it didn't hurt. Gloria leaned on the railing and looked out over the water, and I gathered up all my courage and headed towards her.

She didn't look my way or say anything.

I stopped about a foot from her and leaned on the railing too. "It's nice to get away from all that noise for a bit. Lots of stars tonight." I gazed up at them, but Gloria stared straight ahead her jaw jutted and her chin raised just a little.

"You look really pretty in that black dress, and the pearls are perfect with it," I said.

Gloria turned my way. "Thanks. I made the dress myself."

Her comment gave me just enough bravery to continue. "You don't have to tell me if you don't want to, Gloria, but I noticed you seemed angry during my speech at the banquet. Did I say something wrong?"

Gloria pushed herself away from the railing. She stood there a moment, her lips pursed, as if she was deciding whether to say something or not. Then her words spewed out in a fury. "I'm angry because high school is over, and you and your cool friends made it miserable."

I was so struck by her accusation that I physically took a step back. "But Gloria, I've never even really talked to you till tonight."

"Exactly!"

"What's that supposed to mean?"

She shrugged. "You popular kids are so full of yourselves."

"I'm not a popular kid."

"You take it for granted, so you don't even realize it. But you barely noticed the kids like me who came from Mexico, except maybe to make fun of how we couldn't speak English properly and how we dress."

"But Gloria, you always look cool, and you speak English beautifully."

"Do you know how hard that was? I was nine when my family moved to Canada, but because of my language skills they put me in grade one, with kids three years younger! I felt like a freak! I used to go to the furniture store after school to watch the televisions and hear people speak English properly. Eventually I learned to speak better than my parents and started answering phones for my dad's concrete business. I made enough money to buy magazines and studied makeup and fashion so I could look more 'normal' and fit in at school. But I never did. For twelve years, I've felt like an outsider, no matter how well I speak, or how hard I study, or how good I look."

"Did I ever make fun of you?"

"Probably not, but you didn't stop kids who did. When you gave that speech tonight, you thanked everyone for being so great and supporting you and making high school fun. I was mad. You had support, but you didn't support me or the other immigrant kids or, for that matter, anyone else who was a little different that you. You froze us out."

I didn't know what to say.

Gloria looked at me defiantly. "I'm going away next year. I've been hiding some of the money from my after-school job. My parents don't know it, but I've got a plane ticket to Paris. I'm going someplace where being from Latin America isn't looked down upon. I'm going to get out of Rocky Creek and away from the likes of you. You never even really noticed me before tonight. I'm not sure why you bothered now."

Gloria turned on her heel and strode down the deck. She wobbled just a little, probably from the waves, but she held her head high.

I WAS quiet on the ride back to Rocky Creek. As Annemarie and George snored in the back seat, Levi turned up the music and rolled down his window so he could stay awake.

I wasn't sleepy. All I could think about was what Gloria had said.

Had I really been such a snob? I thought I was a nice person, but did I ever go out of my way to talk to Gloria or the other kids from Latin America? I'd had a locker right in between Annemarie and Dina and we'd always had so much to catch up on between classes. While we giggled and chattered away, were Gloria and her friends watching us and wishing we'd included them in our conversation?

I thought about the senior class trip to New Orleans. I remembered Rod, the boy with big black glasses and horrible acne. He sat in the back of the bus alone most of the time with his nose in a book. Why hadn't I gone to sit with him?

And how about Shelley, the girl with cystic fibrosis who missed school a lot and coughed all the time? I organized the Student Council fundraiser for the Cystic Fibrosis Foundation, but did I ever invite Shelley to a party at my house?

I thought about Marnie, the Cree girl the Dennison family adopted. Maybe I told her I liked her painting at the art show, but did I ever ask her to come to Mike's Cafe to hang out after school?

I closed my eyes when we turned off the Trans-Canada and headed east towards Rocky Creek. But I couldn't sleep. My mind was somersaulting all over the place. I thought I'd been a nice girl in high school, pleasant to everyone. But to Gloria, I hadn't seemed pleasant at all. I'd ignored her and lots of other kids too—acted as if they didn't even exist—and I'd done it without even realizing it or thinking about it.

When we'd driven into the city earlier tonight, we'd gone right past my elementary school in St. Boniface where I'd been in grade one. I thought about all the times I'd had to sit in the hall because I wasn't a Catholic, while the other kids took catechism with the priest. I thought about how I'd choke down fish sandwiches on Friday so I'd fit in, and the way the kids spoke French on the playground and I couldn't understand them. Most of the time, it seemed like I didn't really belong at that school. It stung.

Is that how Gloria had felt?

WE GOT back to Rocky Creek at five in the morning. Levi dropped off Annemarie and George first and then drove me home. I opened the passenger side door. Levi said, "I'll call you tomorrow. Hope your grad was as wonderful as you dreamed it would be, Laura."

I could have said, "No it wasn't," and told Levi what happened with Gloria, but I didn't. I couldn't.

I took the door key out from under the pot of pansies on the porch and let myself into the house as quietly as I could. I kicked off my gold shoes in the foyer and tiptoed upstairs to my room. I could hear Dad snoring, but as I passed the bathroom, I noticed light shining under the door. I opened it to find Mom holding a stack of towels. Contents from the bathroom cupboards lay all over the floor.

"What are you doing, Mom?"

"Just cleaning in here. I've been meaning to do it for a while now, and I couldn't sleep thinking about you, so I decided there was no time like the present. How did it go, Laura? Did you have a nice time?"

"Oh, Mom," I said, and I started to cry.

"What is it? Did you get hurt? Did you and Levi break up? Did you have a car accident? Did you and Annemarie have a fight?"

I shook my head and slid down onto the floor, my back against the bathroom wall, my beautiful grad dress crumpling beneath me. Mom slid down too and put her arm around my shoulders.

"Now, tell me all about it. Every detail."

25

Birthday

WILL

GLORIA IS on my mind all week. In high school, she had felt left out and lonely because she'd been ignored. In elementary school, I'd felt left out and lonely because I'd been bullied.

It's my thirteenth Wednesday going to Grandma's. I've sure liked hearing her stories. I've seen how the stuff that happened to her in the sixties really changed her. Are the things that are happening to me right now doing that too?

My birthday is this Friday. Dad said we'd reconsider me staying home alone after I turn twelve. I wonder what my parents have decided.

Emmaline and Aneesh had planned to come along with me again to Grandma's today, but when I get to our usual spot at the basketball court after school, they aren't there. My heart sinks a bit. Then I see a note on the bench where we usually sit. It's anchored down with rocks. I smile at Emmaline's artistic lettering and the way she's decorated the paper with a border of musical notes and soccer balls. *Had a last-minute change of plans. Meet you at your grandma's.*

I TURN the key in Grandma's lock and open the door.

"Surprise!"

I stagger backwards. Grandma's apartment is filled with people.

"Happy Birthday, Will!" they shout together.

I'm so shocked, I let out a full-throated laugh.

Grandma gives me a hug. "We arranged a little early birthday party for you, William. I hope you don't mind."

"This is great!"

Even Mom and Dad have gotten off work early to come to the party.

"I got a colleague to teach my class today," Mom explains, giving me a hug. "Happy Birthday, Will."

"We did a pretty good job of keeping your party a secret, didn't we, Will?" Emmaline smiles.

"I know I can trust you and Aneesh to keep secrets." I hold up my hand and we high five.

Aneesh slings an arm around my shoulder. "Happy birthday, Will. Didn't get you a gift or anything, but I'm here."

"Only gift I need," I say, turning away before Aneesh can see how close to tears I am.

Grandma's whole living room is hung with balloons. I smell spaghetti and meatballs on the stove. A chocolate cake with twelve candles is in the centre of the dining room table.

Leon and Mendelssohn are here too, and Mendelssohn howls along when everyone sings "Happy Birthday" to me.

Leon hands me an envelope. I pull out three tickets to a concert his symphony is putting on with Carol Jantsch, this outrageous tuba player from Philadelphia. "Your grandmother told me you might have a couple of friends you could bring along." Leon winks.

"Thanks so much, Leon. What a cool gift."

After I've blown out my candles, Grandma gives me her present. "Just so you know, William. I talked to your mom and dad about buying this and they agreed I could."

I tear off the wrapping paper and find the latest iPhone. "Wow! Grandma! This is amazing!"

Mom folds her napkin and carefully lays it by her plate. "We were very impressed with the way you handled the emergency when Grandma was hurt, Will. You acted so maturely we thought you were ready for the responsibility of having your own phone."

Dad clears his throat. "And another thing, Will. We've decided starting next week you can stay home alone on Wednesdays after school."

"That's great, Dad." I push my glasses up my nose and straighten my shoulders. "But if it's okay with Grandma, I think I might still drop by here on the occasional Wednesday."

Dad raises his eyebrows. "If you text us on your new phone after school so we know where you will be, you can choose whether to go home or come to Grandma's."

Mom looks at Grandma. "How do you feel about that arrangement?"

"It is just fine with me." Grandma cracks a huge smile.

"Do you mind if Aneesh and I tag along sometimes?" Emmaline asks.

"I'd love that!" Grandma replies.

When we are ready to leave at the end of the evening Grandma gives me one of her squeeze-as-tight-as-you-can hugs, and I whisper, "There is a postcard from Paris in the suitcase. That's what I want to hear about next time."

Grandma smiles. "I thought you might. Can I expect you next Wednesday then, William?"

"I can hardly wait."

Historical Notes

Chapter 2

- In July 1959, Queen Elizabeth II and Prince Philip visited Winnipeg as part of a Canadian tour.

- Dick and Jane were the main characters in educational texts used to teach children to read in most English-speaking countries from 1930 to 1973.

- At one point in the 1960s, more than 60,000 Catholic nuns worked as teachers, nurses, and social workers in Canada.

- Wooden clappers were a disciplinary tool used by teaching nuns in Canada. They consisted of two pieces of hinged wood that made a clapping noise when brought together. One is in the collection of the Musée de la civilisation in Quebec City.

- Most women's stockings had back seams in 1960. After that, fashions changed, and women began to wear seamless stockings.

Chapter 4

- More than one million Canadians served in the military during the Second World War. This included 50,000 women. Forty-five thousand Canadian soldiers died in the conflict.

- The number of Canadian women holding permanent jobs doubled during the Second World War. At one point, 400,000 women worked in factories.

- *The Cricket in Times Square* by George Seldon was a Newbery Honor book for children published in 1960.

- "O Canada" was originally written in French in 1880 and translated into English in 1906. Although it did not officially become Canada's national anthem until 1980, it was a well-known song in the 1960s and was sung at Remembrance Day ceremonies and other events. The words "in all thy sons command" became part of the lyrics during the First World War. Before that, the phrase used was "thou dost in us command." In 2018, it was officially changed to "in all of us command."

- In the 1960s, almost every school classroom in Canada had a portrait of Queen Elizabeth II displayed prominently.

Chapter 6

- In 1961, the commemoration of the centennial of the birth of the Mohawk poet Emily Pauline Johnson, Tekahionwake, created new interest in her work. She gained recognition as an important Canadian cultural figure. A stamp was issued in her honour.

- Envoy was an automobile brand from General Motors of Canada. The cars were made in England and sold on the Canadian market from 1959 to 1970.

- During the 1960s, the use of snowmobiles became widespread in Canada. Before that, transportation over snow had been impossible except on skis or snowshoes, or by dogsled.

Chapter 8

- The Cuban Missile Crisis lasted from October 16 to November 29, 1962. Escalating tensions between the United States and Russia brought the world the closest it's ever come to all out nuclear war. During the 1960s, schools trained students to duck under their desks and cover their heads to prepare for an attack. In 1962, school evacuation drills were practised across Canada.

- The first yo-yo craze swept through North America in the 1930s. The advent of television advertising in the 1960s exposed some 40 million children ages six to seventeen in the United States to the toy. Forty-five million yo-yos were sold in 1962. They were equally popular in Canada, and yo-yo demonstrations were common on school grounds.

- Spam is a brand of canned pork that gained worldwide popularity after the Second World War. During the war, it provided affordable meat rations for soldiers and the citizens of countries ravaged by the war.

- Many towns and cities in Canada had sirens installed during the Second World War to warn residents of potential air raids. In the 1960s, some communities still sounded the sirens at noon, six o'clock, and nine o'clock to tell children it was time to head home for meals or bed. During the Cold War, the sirens were tested as a means of warning people of a possible nuclear attack.

- The "Flip" was a hairstyle that defined the 1960s. It was made popular by prominent public figures like Jackie Kennedy and Mary Tyler Moore.

Chapter 9

- Woodstock was a 1969 music festival held on a farm in New York that attracted more than 400,000 attendees.

Chapter 10

- The United States president John F. Kennedy was assassinated in Dallas, Texas, on November 22, 1963.

- Lester B. Pearson became the prime minister of Canada in June of 1963.

- In 1956, Neilson's Dairy began distributing free maps of Canada to schools across the country. These maps were a fixture in Canadian classrooms for decades.

- In 1941, the four western provinces of BC, Alberta, Saskatchewan, and Manitoba cooperated in a shared school radio program that included music classes. These were broadcast by CBC Radio and continued until the early 1970s.

- Mary Janes were a popular shoe style for girls in the 1960s. They had a single strap, round toe, and a short, chunky heel.

Chapter 12

- *Ship of Fools*, by Katherine Anne Porter, was a bestselling novel in 1962.

- Before the Second World War, owning or renting a cottage at a lake was something only the wealthiest Canadians could afford. In the 1950s, though, a growing middle class combined with an increased number of paved roads and rural highways made the joys of cottaging accessible to a much larger part of the population.

Chapter 14

- It wasn't until 1967 that the idea of teaching sex education or reproductive health in schools was introduced in Canada.

- *Seventeen* was a magazine for teenage girls first published in 1944. In the 1960s, its covers often featured famous Hollywood stars like Rock Hudson.

Chapter 16

- The Vietnam War lasted from 1954 to 1975. It is estimated that up to 2 million Vietnamese civilians, as well as 1.1 million North Vietnamese and Viet Cong fighters and between 200,000 and 250,000 South Vietnamese soldiers, were killed in the conflict. By the end of 1966, American forces in Vietnam reached 385,000 troops plus an additional 60,000 sailors stationed offshore. More than 6,000 Americans were killed that year and 30,000 wounded. Between 20,000 and 30,000 Americans entered Canada illegally during the height of the war in order to escape being drafted into the conflict. They were known as "draft dodgers." The war was extremely controversial in the United States, and the antiwar movement is associated with many of the cultural touchstones we associate with the 1960s today.

- The use of seatbelts only became mandatory in 1984 in Canada.

- *The Fugitive* was a popular television series from 1963 to 1967 about a doctor on the run after he is wrongfully accused of this wife's murder.

- The Mercury Marquis was a line of cars marketed by the Ford Motor company. It sold from 1967 to 1986.

Chapter 18

- Appetite suppression products became very popular in the 1960s. Most of them were eventually found to have dangerous side-effects. They were withdrawn from the pharmaceutical market—but not before they had been prescribed to millions of women, for weight-loss purposes.

- Manitoba did not ban smoking in public places like restaurants until 2004.

- The two-dollar bill was issued by the Bank of Canada from 1935 to 1996.

- The movie *Romeo and Juliet*, a romantic tragedy based on the Shakespeare play of the same name, debuted in 1968. It was very popular with teenagers because it was the first film to use actors that were the same age as the characters in the original play. Olivia Hussey won a Golden Globe for her performance.

- Twiggy was an British teenager who became a famous model during the 1960s. She was known for her thin build, big eyes, and short hair.

- Expo 67 was an international exhibition or World's Fair held in Montreal, Quebec, from June to October of 1967. It attracted nearly 55 million visitors.

Chapter 20

- In Canada, dishwashers did not become common household appliances until the 1970s. Before that, their cost was too high for many families to afford.

- The Ford Motor Company included complimentary 8-track tapes in all their vehicles from 1965 to 1974, each year producing a new one featuring a variety of music.

- It was only at the end of the 1990s that technology made it possible to aim radiation for cancer more precisely. Before that, it was hard to control radiation from reaching normal tissue while delivering a high enough dose to kill cancer.

- The Rodgers and Hammerstein number "You'll Never Walk Alone" became very popular in the sixties when Gerry and the Pacemakers, a young British band from Liverpool, recorded the song and sent it rocketing up the music charts.

Chapter 22

- In 1969, there were approximately 400,000 farms in Canada.

- In the 1960s, bell-bottom pants became fashionable for both men and women. Commonly made of denim, they flared out from the bottom of the calf and were often worn with boots.

- The Studebaker car company began producing vehicles in 1902. The last Studebaker car came off the assembly line in Hamilton, Ontario, in 1966.

Chapter 24

- The *Paddlewheel Princess* was a boat built in 1966 that plied Manitoba rivers for some forty years. It was the setting for hundreds of high school graduation parties.

- A common education practice in the 1960s was to put new immigrant children arriving in Canada into grade one no matter their age. They were only allowed to progress to subsequent grades as their English improved.

- During the 1960s, hundreds of Indigenous children were removed from their families and communities of birth and adopted into white middle-class families across Canada. This is called the "Sixties Scoop."

- "I Feel the Earth Move," by Carole King, was released in April of 1971 and became the biggest mainstream pop hit of the year.

Acknowledgements

MY SON is a professional musician and a few years ago, my husband, Dave, and I were waiting in line outside for the venue doors to open before a concert by his band, Royal Canoe. It started to rain and Dave remarked to the young people around us, "This reminds me of Woodstock." They all looked at him with blank stares. Obviously, none of them knew anything about the memorable thunderstorm at the famous Woodstock music festival in 1969. That incident had me wondering if perhaps there weren't lots of things the current generation of kids didn't know about the sixties. Could I write a book that would introduce them to the era of my childhood and teen years in a way that would be relevant and meaningful? With *Sixties Girl*, I've tried to do just that.

This novel would not have been published without Deborah Froese, who is both an accomplished professional editor and my friend. She guided me through a major rewrite of the original manuscript. Her astute criticism and constant encouragement were indispensable. I can't thank her enough.

I have dedicated this novel to my siblings Kaaren Neufeld, Ken Peters, and Mark Peters, who shared family life with me during the 1960s. They were all initial readers of the early drafts of my manuscript and offered words of wisdom and advice that guided me as I continued to work on *Sixties Girl*.

As always, the group of Manitoba children's writers who I have been meeting with for almost a decade provided valuable feedback and affirmation. Thanks to Jodi Carmichael, Deborah Froese, Gabriele Goldstone, Larry Verstraete, Pat Trottier, Christina Jantz, Melanie Matheson, Mindi Marshall, Suzanne Golden, and Candice Sareen.

I also want to thank the readers of my first novel, *Lost on the Prairie*. I've had the pleasure of speaking with hundreds of you at different events where I was repeatedly encouraged to write another book. This new novel is not really a sequel to *Lost on the Prairie*, but Laura and Will in *Sixties Girl* are the granddaughter and great-great grandson of Peter, the hero of *Lost on the Prairie*.

I know I will be asked if this book is a work of fiction and it truly is, although many events in Laura's life were at least partially inspired by my own experiences. My Dad did take me up on the roof of the St. Boniface Hospital to see Queen Elizabeth in the summer of 1959; I memorized the poem "The Song My Paddle Sings" in elementary school; and I once witnessed the rescue of a stranded deer from a lake. I danced away the night of my high school graduation on a Winnipeg riverboat, and my family did make a trip to Expo 67. I'd love to come and talk to your book club, school class, church, or community group about my other personal connections to the stories. Most of *Sixties Girl*, however, sprang from my imagination and from research I did about the decade.

I have included notes at the end of the book to explain historical references in each of Laura's stories that younger readers may not know about. In the resource section of my website (maryloudriedger.com), there is a teaching and reading guide for *Sixties Girl*, which provides all kinds of ideas and curricular connections for educators who may want to use the book to explore the sixties decade further with their students. The guide also has materials for talking with kids about bullying and what they can do to deal with it should they have experiences like Will does in the book.

I am endlessly grateful to Heritage House for publishing both of my books. Thank you especially to Lara Kordic, Nandini Thaker, Monica Miller, and Setareh Ashrafologhalai for their work on *Sixties Girl*.

Finally, I want to acknowledge the love, support, and interest of my friends and family, in particular my husband Dave, my children Joel Dreidger and Karen Leis, and Bucky Dreidger and Alisa Wiebe, and my grandchildren Henri, Leo, Clementine, and Nora Dot.

About the Author

MARYLOU DRIEDGER'S curiosity and love of learning have taken her to some fifty destinations across the globe. She is currently employed as an educator at the Winnipeg Art Gallery but prior to that taught for four decades in a variety of schools in three different countries.

MaryLou is the recipient of a Manitoba Teacher of the Year award. Her best-selling novel *Lost on the Prairie* was nominated for the Eileen McTavish Award for Best First Book (Manitoba Book Awards, 2022) and the Manitoba Young Readers' Choice Awards, Sundogs (2023). She has been a columnist for the *Winnipeg Free Press* and *The Carillon*, and her freelance work has been published in numerous periodicals, anthologies, travel guides, institutional histories, and curriculums. MaryLou chronicles her adventures on her popular daily blog, maryloudriedger2.wordpress.com.